WHISPERS IN THE WILDERNESS

WHISPERS IN THE WILDERNESS

WHISPERS IN THE WILDERNESS

Frontier Brides, Book 2

Colleen L Reece

CHIVERS

British Library Cataloguing in Publication Data available

This Large Print edition published by AudioGO Ltd, Bath, 2012.
Published by arrangement with the Author

U.K. Hardcover   ISBN   978 1 4458 2670 7
U.K. Softcover   ISBN   978 1 4458 2671 4

Scripture quotations are taken from the King James Version of the Bible.

Printed and bound in Great Britain by
MPG Books Group Limited

CHAPTER 1

Go or stay? Joel Scott slid from the saddle of his ebony mare, Querida, and let the reins drop. Trained to stand, she whinnied, rubbed her soft nose against his shoulder, then began to graze; the rise overlooking the Double J was no stranger to her.

A pang went through this golden-haired man with the face of an angel. How could he leave northern Arizona and all it offered? He gazed into the valley below — mute but appealing, it lay like a crumpled blanket carelessly tossed by a giant hand. Hills, valleys, forested slopes, and the distant rims of red canyons — they all wove invisible webs, as they had done eleven summers ago when Joel and his aunt ended their long search for Uncle Gideon. How quickly the years had flown! The seven-year-old boy, who had whooped with excitement when he first saw the Double J, lurked inside Joel's heart. Along with that was the awe that filled him each time he surveyed the now-expanded ranch.

Cloudless Arizona skies smiled, no bluer than the keen eyes of the motionless man. Quaking aspens with their greenish-white trunks bent toward one another and whispered wilderness gossip. Pine, cedar, and grass rustled, alive with the sheer joy of summer.

"I can't go." Joel did not realize he had spoken aloud until Querida abandoned her grazing to nuzzle his arm. He sighed and buried his face in her black mane. Even if he could bear to leave the ranch and his family, how could he part with Querida? Ten years earlier, Gideon had called his nephew to the barn. "One of the mares is ready to foal. You need to be there."

Joel wondered at the mysterious look in his uncle's face but obediently trotted after the tall man he resembled. Even now he could remember every detail of the birth, his first to witness.

"It's a filly," Gideon told the wide-eyed boy. "Male horses are colts. She's yours, Son."

"Mine?" Joel had ridden various Double J horses, but none had been his very own. He watched the filly struggle to her feet on legs that seemed too long for her body. Within a few hours, she ran about but never strayed far from her mother.

"What shall I call her?" He thought of all the black things he could: Soot, Ink, Dark Cloud. But Aldrich, longtime foreman for Gideon, shook his head. "This filly's gonna become a real pard," he told the excited boy. "Name her something special."

"What?" Joel respected Aldrich for his range lore.

Aldrich's leathery face broke into a smile, and his eyes twinkled. "Once, a long time ago, I had a pretty little filly named Querida. That's Spanish for *beloved.*" He pronounced it *Kay-reeda.*

"Querida." Joel rolled the name around on his tongue, patted his gift, and repeated, "Querida. Beloved." From that moment, the two were inseparable. By the time Querida turned five, she had reached full height and weight.

Twice, she had saved Joel from danger. Once with Joel aboard, she had outrun a visiting outlaw who had tried to buy her and had been refused. The second time was just a few months after Joel's sixteenth birthday, when Joel's foot was painfully twisted and held fast by a rock slide, trapping him. Although her eyes showed that she did not want to leave him, Querida obeyed her master's command to go home. Her arrival at the Double J, without Joel, resulted in a prompt rescue, and he loved her more than ever afterwards.

Joel's mind returned to the present. "God, I don't know what to do." He impulsively turned to his best Friend. "You know I want to serve You — it's all I've ever wanted. To take up Uncle Gideon's work and preach." His heart glowed at the prospect.

In Flagstaff, he had already earned the nickname of the boy preacher, and it was jealously defended by Lonesome, Dusty, Aldrich, and the other Double J hands. Strangers sometimes mistakenly branded Joel as soft until a demonstration of his riding or roping would convince even the strongest nonbeliever that a man could follow God and still be a top cowboy. Talk of his talents ran second only to the ripple of shock that Gideon had caused years before when he laid down his no-drinking rule for the Double J and made it stick because of who he was and the wages he offered.

Once, a new rider asked how come young Scott could talk a bird out of its bush and still be fearless and strong.

"A lot of folks think Jesus was a tenderfoot," the young preacher shot back. "But then, a lot of folks can be wrong." His frank smile took any sting out of his words. "The hills around where Jesus lived are steep and probably as rough as some of our Arizona country. How far do you think a coddled weakling would get trying to climb them?"

The rider scratched his head and allowed that it would not be far.

Ever since his eighteenth birthday, on the last day of April, Joel found himself more introspective than ever. That day, he learned the full story of his past. Joel had always known his mama died and Aunt Judy raised him. When he inquired about his real father and why he never knew him, Gideon and Judith simply said, "When you're a man, Son, we'll tell you everything." The pain in their faces stilled his boyish questions, but the feeling of some dark secret haunted him. Two years after he and Judith came to the Double J in 1877, twin cousins came along, Matt and Millie. Judith beckoned ten-year-old Joel to see the babies and told him, "They'll be more like your brother and sister than cousins, Joel, Dear." Her dark eyes shone. "I'll need you to help me a great deal now." His childish heart swelled with the trust he saw in her face, and by the time they could toddle, Joel had the twins riding in front of him.

As if conjured up by his thoughts of them, a high-pitched cry shattered the peaceful time of contemplation. "Joel!" It echoed from a nearby cliff wall but died in the steady beat of hooves when Matt and Millie burst into sight and raced toward him. How those eight-year-olds could ride! Pride rose in the waiting man and chased away the need for solitude. Since April, he had mulled over the unvarnished facts of his birth. How Cyrus Scott, unworthy of the favoritism of his father, had fallen in love with pretty Millicent Butler, married her using his brother Gideon's name, then gone away without knowing of Joel's coming.

"Are you sure he didn't know about me?" Joel had demanded when the sad story ended.

"He never knew." Judith's lips trembled. "In the message I sent to him, I only said that Millie had died."

"Then he abandoned Mama but not me," Joel said, feeling somewhat relieved.

"He also said he was sorry and asked for forgiveness," Gideon put in. Longing filled his face. "I always wanted to go back, to try again to find my brother. . . ."

Did the idea begin then? Joel wondered. The passionate longing to somehow repay the wronged uncle who rode away in bitterness when his father would not believe him innocent? Months and years had passed before God's perfect timing brought Gideon and Judith together to marry and confess the love that grew during their separation.

He would be following a cold trail, common sense advised him. *With God all things are possible* (Mark 10:27), Joel's heart retorted.

Gideon could never go. A few months before Joel and Judith had come, Gideon had been shot. The doctor who had attended him had predicted that Gideon would always walk with a limp and that riding for too long or hard would result in pain. Although he managed well, a familiar grimace of pain showed Joel the folly of his uncle's attempting the kind of riding that would be necessary in traveling the path back to the past.

The second part of Gideon's dream was to return to Tomkinsville, Colorado, where he had traveled under Cyrus's name and had fallen into gambling. "There are so many I want to tell about Jesus," he said brokenly. His strong face worked, and Joel felt his own heart bound with sympathy. Joel almost cried out that he would take Gideon's place, but caution sealed his lips. Not until he received orders from his heavenly Father could he make such a commitment.

Yes, he had considered much since April. A few more days would not matter. He hailed the twins, laughingly declared their race as ended in a tie, then mounted Querida, and rode home, a chattering child on each side. But the aspens and pines and cedars continued their tattletale whispering and filled the wilderness with soft sounds, which were increased by the early evening breeze that sprang up and set the leaves to fluttering even more.

Day after day, Joel continued helping with the endless ranch chores, his perfectly trained body busy with his tasks and his mind free to consider. To his amazement, once the unspoken idea of retracing Gideon's journey came, it settled in like butter on a hot biscuit. Suppose he could find his real father. Surely the message his father had sent to the family's Circle S ranch showed repentance! Would not Cyrus Scott's heart be softened if the son he never knew sought him out? Finally, Joel realized why the idea appealed to him so much.

"Lord, I don't want my father to die without knowing You." He paused but refused to think of all he would leave behind if he rode away from home. "Before I go, I need to know if this is just what I want or if it's Your will."

Joel settled into a time of waiting, and the knowledge that he should go firmed. Still, he hesitated, testing himself and praying for something — anything — that would justify his decision. His answer came like a clap of thunder.

One sunny afternoon, Tomkins, who had befriended Gideon so long ago, brought Judith and Joel west, then bought into the Double J and helped it grow, rode out from his home in Flagstaff. Married to a fine woman whose husband had died on their journey to Arizona, Tomkins divided his time between the ranch and various business enterprises in town. "This state will grow," he had predicted. "It's 1888, the Indian fighting's over since Geronimo surrendered a couple of years back, and the Southern Pacific Railroad's bringing more folks in all the time. Ranching, mining, farming — Arizona's got them all."

Always cheerful and forward-looking, Tomkins had lost some of his pleasant expression this afternoon. Finally, he admitted sheepishly, "I guess my foot's getting itchy. I have a hankering to see Colorado at least once more. It was mighty good to me."

A wistful look came into his keen eyes. "My wife's sister's been pestering her to visit her in California, and I've been thinking about heading east for a spell while she's gone." He lifted an eyebrow. "Only thing is, it'd be a lot more enjoyable if I had a traveling companion. What are the chances of Joel going with me?"

Thank You, Lord. Joel felt his last doubt slide away. "How are you going?"

"I'm game to just ride a horse and forget all the newfangled ways to travel," Tomkins drawled. "I reckon that Querida mare of yours can carry you to Colorado."

"And to Texas."

"Texas! Who said anything about Texas?" Tomkins's eyebrows arched like an angry cat's back.

"Texas?" Gideon's eyes gleamed, and he leaned forward. "What's on your mind, Joel?" His hands clenched and unclenched.

Joel's fiery blue gaze met his uncle's. "I want to go back to San Scipio and see my grandparents. Then, I'm going to find my father."

"You mean *try* to find him, don't you?" Judith looked shocked but sympathetic. The years had been kind to her; not a single gray hair marred the dark braids she still wore in a coronet.

16

"No. I'll stay until I find him."

"Impossible!" Yet, the hope in Gideon's face outweighed his words. "I tried everything. It's been fourteen years."

"Have you considered how little chance there is of your succeeding?" Judith quietly asked.

"Aunt Judy." The childish nickname came naturally. "I can't even remember the first time you taught me that God can do anything and that we must have faith." Joel straightened to his full six-foot height, young in build but with a man's steady determination in his face. "Ever since my birthday, I've known I have to find my father if he is still alive." The last words came in a whisper.

"Then you have my blessing. I only wish I were going with you," Gideon confessed. He held out a strong hand and gripped Joel's. "When you stop at the Circle S, tell Dad and Mother we already have a wing planned for them if they ever decide to sell out and come to Arizona."

"I will." As easily as that, Joel left the crossroads he had tarried beside for weeks. What lay ahead? Only God knew. He looked into Millie's and Matt's faces, quiet for once, awed by the serious grown-up talk. His gaze traveled to Gideon's face and noted the mingled fear of failure and unquenchable hope. Then to Judith, whose tranquil posture reassured him. He had known leaving would be hard, but he had not counted on its being such a wrench. All the years with Judith danced before him — the loving care, the sacrifices.

Did she sense his feelings? A small smile tilted her lips up. "God will go with you, Joel. Remember, your name means *Jehovah is the Lord.*"

This brittle moment, one to treasure, was broken by Millie's plaintive, "Aren't you *ever* coming back, Joel?"

"Of course I will." He smiled at her, and her anxious look faded. Yet, when good nights had been said and Joel restlessly sought out Querida, he wondered, *How many weeks and months, even years, might it be before I return to the Double J?* He set his lips in a narrow line and vowed, "God, You have blessed my family with the means to let me go. I am going in Your name, to set things straight for Uncle Gideon and to carry salvation to those along the way. Especially to my father. Please, ride with me. No, let me ride with You — until I find my father."

News of Joel's departure created an uproar on the Double J. "Just when I'm gettin' ya

18

to be worth somethin', you ups and rides out," Lonesome complained. Eleven years had not changed the irrepressible cowboy who now owned stock and shares in the ranch. "Dawgone, but it don't pay to invest time in a feller."

"Aw, stop your bellyachin'," Dusty called. "Everyone knows it was me who taught Joel what he knows."

"Sez who?" Lonesome ruffled like a turkey.

"Sez me."

Joel took advantage of their good-natured warfare to escape. The last thing he needed was to let the outfit know how big a lump lay in his chest. Knowing he had to go did not make it easier. Neither did uncertainty as to when he would be back . . . if ever.

From the moment Joel declared his intention to go with Tomkins, Gideon made time to spend with his nephew. With their fair heads bent over roughly drawn maps, they endlessly discussed the route that had brought Gideon from Colorado to Arizona.

"Here's a list of folks whose names I remember," the older man said, eyes filled with a reminiscent light. "People who offered a bed or a bite to eat and never asked for a peso." He laughed gleefully, and some of the lines that the years had etched dis-

19

appeared from his face. "I used to hide some money where they'd find it after I left. Always felt like a kid with a new toy, thinking about the way they'd look when they found it."

He hesitated, then said, "Joel, there are two in particular I hope you can find. The girl Lily. I helped her get out of the saloon, but I didn't tell her about God." The laughter left his face, and he looked bleak. "The other one's Eb Sears."

"The man you were accused of knifing?" Joel stared.

"Yes. If he had lied, I'd have been sent to prison for a long time. Rough and mean as he was, Eb Sears must have had something good deep down, or he wouldn't have admitted he was drunk and loud, then cleared me of blame." Gideon added, "If I hadn't been so bitter against God, I'd have stayed and tried to work on that hidden good. Tell Sears where I am and that if he ever needs a job, he has one on the Double J — that is, if he will leave the bottle alone!"

A few mornings later, just after daylight but before the sun rose, Tomkins and Joel leisurely rode away from the Double J. By common consent, they halted on top of the rise and looked back. Fog wraiths hovered

20

in the air, waiting for the sun's kiss to dissolve them. Wisps of smoke curled from the ranch house and bunkhouse chimneys. The eternal whispering of the quaking aspens trembled in Joel's ears, calling him back, pushing him on. By the time the travelers reached the high country, the green leaves would be tinged with gold, yellower than the stuff miners sold their souls to possess.

"Whispers in the wilderness," Joel said softly.

"Yeah." Tomkins relaxed in the saddle, then reminded, "It's a long way." His gaze bored into the younger man, whose fair hair showed in front of his pushed-back Stetson and contrasted sharply with Querida's shining dark hide. "It may be an even longer way home."

"I know." Yet, when the sun burst over a hill and flooded the valley with rosy light, Joel knew he would not turn back if he could. Perhaps some of his father's restless blood stirred and came to life.

With a sense of freedom, responsibility, and urgency, he anticipated what lay ahead. His vivid imagination pictured the aspen leaves whispering *hurry, hurry,* and Joel wanted to prod Querida into a dead run. For an instant, a single dark cloud appeared and blocked the sun's rays. Joel shivered.

Again came that feeling of the need to hurry.

Should he tell Tomkins he could not go to Colorado, then strike out alone across Arizona, through New Mexico, and then to San Scipio? Were there forces surrounding the elder Scotts or Cyrus, if he lived, that demanded action and soon?

Do not be a fool, he chided himself. *You felt God confirming your decision to do exactly what you are doing when Tomkins suggested it. You cannot turn back now on the strength of a whim.* Yet, all that first day of travel, Joel found himself anxiously watching the southeastern sky and the giant thunderheads that gathered and attacked the earth. With the ability he had possessed since childhood to sense trouble, he prayed silently but mightily that his quest, his mission, would not fail.

No one could have been a better trailmate than Tomkins. He spoke when Joel wanted to talk, rode quietly when the younger man needed time to think, and he always recognized those times. The same qualities that Gideon had discovered in Tomkins the year they wintered together on the trapline proved strong and welcome now to Joel. Yet, a difference existed. Where Gideon had been embittered and refused to mention

22

God, except to rail against him, Joel shared his early childhood faith. It strengthened them both. Around their nighttime campfires, when shadows hid expressions too private for anyone but God to observe, the men became partners. Joel would have trusted his life to Tomkins. He rejoiced that the older man had accepted Christ shortly after he came to Arizona. They spent hours talking of what the raw West would be like if only God were allowed to be in control, instead of greed and hatred.

Always, Joel carried Gideon's list. As they traveled, name after name received a heavy line through it. Some had moved. Others welcomed the young man with hearty approval and tales of how they discovered his uncle's money in the family Bible or under a plate. Joel's eyes opened wide at the stories. Time after time, those families, who had given what they could little afford to share and who secretly prayed for God's help, received their reward . . . and praised His name for using a passing stranger.

Tomkins's eyes glistened at the stories, and once he gruffly told Joel, "I reckon I had a part in helping answer their prayers, don't you think? If your uncle hadn't grubstaked me, I wouldn't have given him money." He cocked his head. "Wonder how the good Lord would have taken care of those folks in that situation?"

"I've decided I don't have to know *how* or *why* God does things," Joel said soberly. "Just that He does them."

Tomkins grunted, and Joel saw the approving look the other man sent toward him.

The feeling of urgency lessened a bit as they worked their way toward Tomkinsville. They had tarried along the way, and before they had reached the high country, fall had had the opportunity to paint the leaves with its frosty brush. Joel felt he had come home when they climbed the hills and saw his old friends, the quaking aspens. Now, their whispering leaves shone butter yellow, and with each passing breeze, some dropped to the ground to huddle in great golden piles. Miles of wilderness, broken only by a deserted cabin here and there, offered peace and a time to prepare for what lay ahead.

"It might be a ghost town," Tomkins muttered when they mounted the last hill from where they could look down into town. "I haven't kept in touch. Mining may be over."

Joel heard dread in his companion's voice and said nothing, but his heart thumped against his ribs. Tomkinsville represented the place where his real work must begin — the work of taking the gospel of Jesus Christ to those who most needed it and least realized their need.

"Aw, look at that!" A sigh of relief from Tomkins blended with a blast of loud music. "Still here and it sounds the same." He craned his neck, and Joel rode up beside him where the trail widened. Surrounded by snow-topped mountains, Joel's first parish waited.

CHAPTER 2

A tiny pulse hammered in Joel's temple. Fourteen years earlier, his uncle Gideon had ridden into Tomkinsville, sick at heart and corroded with the bitterness of false accusations. Now, Joel returned as Gideon's emissary. Another blast of raucous music desecrated the peaceful mountain air, and the young man shuddered. Flagstaff with its Saturday night cowboy sprees had been wild, but Tomkinsville roared like a wounded cougar. Would he be equal to the task that lay ahead?

He straightened in the saddle, and Querida softly whinnied. God willing, they would ride straight into the wide-open town and, if it were His plan, stir hearts for Him. Joel wondered how God felt when men invaded some of His most beautiful creations with their schemes and treachery, plotting and sin. Back home, he and Tomkins had seen mountains as high as

26

Humphreys Peak, north of Williams, that reached well over twelve thousand feet. Crowned with early snowcaps, they glistened and shimmered in the distance, everlastingly there as a backdrop for the layers of aspens and dark evergreens that clustered at their feet. Silver waterfalls and tumbling streams fell over rocky ledges, their water so cold Joel's teeth ached when he drank. Did the inhabitants of Tomkinsville ever look up and see the beauty? Or were they too engrossed in their quest for gold and silver, gambling and drinking to raise their gaze above material things?

"First thing we should do is find a place to stay," Tomkins advised. He laughed, but Joel could see excitement in his face. "Funny, not so long ago, folks riding in would have been asking me about lodging!" He shrugged, then shamefacedly admitted, "I guess I had to come back one more time to find out how much I have back in Arizona." He fell silent.

Joel's heart beat with sympathy. What must it be like to have a wife waiting when a man came home? A rush of color streaked his tanned face. Flagstaff had lots of nice girls, but he had never seen one yet that he would want to hitch up with for life. Double harness meant two lives blended into one, each caring for the other. He had learned that from watching Gideon and Judith. They did not have to shout their love from Humphreys Peak to let people know it ran swift as a river in flood.

Tomkins shot him a keen glance. "Someday, Boy, you'll meet a special girl. When you do, make sure she's true and real, not just a pretty face."

Joel marveled again at the way Tomkins often seemed to read his thoughts. "I will." The idea warmed him. "I'll never marry until I know God approves." He felt he had just taken as solemn a vow as marriage itself, but his irrepressible sense of humor made him add, "I've never even courted anyone yet, so I'll hold off getting married for awhile. Besides, there's a long trail ahead."

Tomkins grinned appreciatively and reined in before the same log building that had housed his enterprises years before. No longer new, it hugged the ground firmly. The weathered logs brought a memory of Gideon returning to find that his old friend was now the big man in Tomkinsville. It was a thrilling story, one that Joel had begged to hear dozens of times — how only the inherent honesty of a loud, crude cowboy saved Gideon.

An hour later, the visitors surveyed the snug cabin Tomkins had rented at a price he snorted over and called robbery.

"You're lucky to get it at any price," the smooth-tongued gent in a funeral-black suit told them. "More and more people are coming into town all the time. Only reason I have this cabin available is that its owner took up a new residence."

Something in the man's voice sent a chill up Joel's backbone. "Where?"

"Boot Hill." A wave of the hand toward the window indicated a set-apart area with wildflowers blowing in the wind and a fresh gash in the earth. "The way I heard, he talked when he should have been listening and flashed a roll of bills that would choke a horse. Next morning, the sheriff stumbled over a body. The money hasn't shown up." He abruptly changed the subject. "Do you want it for the winter?"

Joel started to nod, caught Tomkins's warning glance, and stopped. He also saw a gleam in the agent's eyes he did not trust, and when the man asked a shade too casually, "Where did you say you were from?" Joel kept mum.

His trailmate looked squarely into the curious man's face. "We didn't say. By the way, they named this town after me some

29

time back. I guess that's enough. We'll look over these accommodations and let you know."

Doubt replaced the suspicious gleam. The agent backtracked. "If you want the cabin for at least a month, I can let you have it a little cheaper." He named a price, still high.

Tomkins grimaced and threw down the money. "If it's dirty, we'll come back and use you for a floor mop."

Joel's mouth dropped open. He had never seen this side of his friend, not even on the long trip west with Judith years before. The minute they got outside, he burst out with, "You sure stopped him!"

Tomkins's shrewd face gave credence to his words. "Son, this is Tomkinsville." He swung onto his horse, and Joel knew that a far deeper meaning than he had suspected lay beneath the dry comment.

Their new home sat on a rounded rise out of town and far enough away to avoid some of the clamor. A view of distant peaks from the front window, the two small bedrooms with hand-hewn bedsteads, a large living room/kitchen combination, and the semi-privacy of the cabin offered all they needed.

Tomkins's eagle gaze swept over the large room. "It will do for a meeting place until we get enough folks coming to need a bigger building." He brought in a bucket of water from a nearby creek and spluttered when the icy drops hit his face. "Your turn. We don't want to meet Tomkinsville looking like two tumbleweeds."

Joel gasped when he felt the cold water on his dirty, heated skin. His teeth chattered, but he rubbed a rough towel on his face and warmed himself up. The one set of good clothes he had brought came out of his saddlebags clean but wrinkled.

"We'll find a laundry," Tomkins promised. "First, let's go get some grub." He had changed into clean pants and shirt, then bunched his trail clothes into a bundle to take with him.

Joel thought of how they had washed out their garments as best they could on their journey. Twice, a friendly rancher's wife had insisted on doing it. He swiftly made his own bundle of laundry and followed Tomkins out to the horses. "I suppose there's a livery stable here?"

"Huh!" Tomkins's eyes glowed like twin coals. "We'll keep real close watch on our horses, especially yours. No livery stable for Querida. Some of the men around here used to have taking ways and probably still do."

They found a small eating place and

gorged on fresh beefsteak, mashed potatoes and gravy, corn, biscuits as light as Judith had ever made, and two pieces of apple pie apiece. Black coffee, strong enough to float a lead bar, finished off the meal.

"Well, are you ready for Tomkinsville?"

Joel took a long breath. "If it's ready for me!" he told his friend.

"Now, don't go doing anything stupid," Tomkins warned when they reached the noisy main street. They strolled along until they reached the Missing Spur Saloon. Joel's unfamiliarity with such places left him wide-eyed and wondering why Tomkins would choose a saloon as the place for making their presence known.

"There's bound to be some here who'll remember me." The answer to his unspoken question steadied Joel. "Let me do the talking." He pushed ahead of Joel and stepped inside.

The younger man's first impression mingled color and light, the reek of booze, cigarette and cigar smoke, too-loud laughter, and rough language. For a moment, he felt he had been there before. Then he realized that a replica of Gideon's descriptions, complete in every detail, lay before him. A few heads turned toward the strangers, surveyed them, then went back to their gambling and drinking.

"Don't I know you?" A burly man shouldered his way from the long bar and confronted them.

"You should. I sold you your first horse," Tomkins said.

"Well, by the powers, if it ain't Tomkins himself!" The rough face broke apart into a wide smile. "I hear tell you've been down Arizony way." He clapped Tomkins on the back. "Set 'em up, boys. This is the feller who begun what made this town famous!"

A roar of approval went up. Men crowded toward the bar, but Tomkins stopped them with the wave of a hand. "Sorry, men. I don't drink."

Guffaws replaced the cheers; scowls erased smiles.

"You ain't serious!" The burly man stared. "What'd you do, git religion?"

"That's about it." Tomkins did not move a muscle. Joel had never been prouder of his friend.

"Well, I'll be . . ." The man's jaw sagged. "What about your friend?" He turned toward Joel.

"He —"

Joel cut in, unwilling to be announced as a preacher at this particular moment. "I don't drink, either. I'm looking for a man."

Stone-cold, dead silence filled the hazy room. Tomkins's acquaintance's eyes narrowed to slits. "An' who might that man be?"

Joel sensed a certain breathlessness and rushed in where the devil himself would have hesitated. "Name of Eb Sears."

"What!" The thunderstruck man shook his head as if he had not heard right. "Why in tarnation does a kid like you come marchin' in lookin' for Sears?"

"He and my uncle had a mix-up years ago, and —"

"Shut up, Joel!" Tomkins seized his arm with a steel grip.

Bewildered and unsure of what he had done but instinctively knowing it was wrong, Joel felt himself propelled back toward the door. An angry buzzing, like tormented bees from a hive, followed him. Just then the door flew inward, narrowly missing Joel. A heavyset man, carrying the smell of horse, stepped inside. He raised one eyebrow curiously at the sight of a young stranger being pushed toward the door.

"Hey, Sears, the kid's lookin' for you," someone called. "Says you and his uncle had trouble years ago. Think you c'n handle him?" A roar of mocking laughter rocked the room.

34

Tomkins muttered something under his breath, released Joel, and took one step to the side. "Hello, Eb."

Sears shifted his astonished gaze. "Tomkins! What're you doin' back here? And who is this kid? He looks like someone I know." He glanced back at Joel. "Who's his uncle, and hadn't you better be in bed, Sonny? It's gettin' kinda late for you to be up, ain't it?"

Eager to deliver Gideon's message, Joel ignored both the fresh round of laughter and Tomkins's muttered, "Get out of here." He asked, "Remember the name Cyrus Scott?"

"Scott? Yeah, the guy they said knifed me but didn't." Sears shook himself, and his brows met in puzzlement. "I cleared him. So how come you're lookin' for me a bunch of years later?" He dropped one hand suggestively to his gun butt. Then suspicion wiped out confusion, and he jerked his revolver out of its holster.

Before it cleared leather, Sears found himself looking straight into the steady muzzle of Joel's pistol.

"Who are you, Kid?" Sears's face turned the color of old wax. "Only man I ever saw who could draw that fast was Scott."

"Put the gun on the table." Joel gestured,

35

his face set. What a horrible way to attract the attention of Tomkinsville! He sheathed his own gun and held out his right hand. "Sears, I'm Joel Scott, Gideon Scott's nephew."

"I don't know no Gideon Scott, just Cyrus." Some of the color seeped back into Sears's ruddy face, but he didn't take the outstretched hand.

"My uncle used that name then," Joel explained. His voice sounded loud and strange in the silent room. "He has a big ranch in northern Arizona, the Double J. He got shot up years back and can't ride the way he wants to. I've come to Tomkinsville to shake your hand, tell you he's never forgotten how you told the truth and saved him, and to let you know if you ever need a riding job, there's a place for you on the Double J."

A concerted gasp ran through the room. Sears stepped back as if shocked, then stretched out his hand and grumbled, "What a way to bring friendly greetin's." He gripped Joel's hands. "We mighta killed each other."

"Naw," a heckler called while feet shifted and onlookers sat back in their chairs. "He'da bored ya, if he wanted, Eb. Young feller, where'd ya learn to shoot like that?"

"From his uncle," Tomkins interjected. He sounded delighted at the way things had turned out, but the low note in his voice told Joel he was in for it when they got home. "Well, boys, now that you've all seen what Scott can do, I'd like to invite you to see some more of his skills."

"Can he ride? Rope?" Sears shot a significant look at Tomkins. Tomkins laughed, nodded, and said loud enough for every person present to hear, "Yeah. Preach, too." His enjoyment of the situation spilled over, and his eyes twinkled. "Come out to the old Furman cabin on Sunday morning. He preaches as good as he draws a gun."

Shock, mirth, and disbelief warred in the faces of Sears and several men who crowded around him. "This kid a *preacher?* Some of the rocks you dug looking for gold musta slipped and hit you on the head," Sears pronounced solemnly.

"If you don't believe me, come see for yourself." Tomkins nudged Joel.

Joel flashed his heartwarming smile. "Sorry I had to pull a gun on you, Mr. Sears. I had to make sure you didn't kill me before I could give you Gideon's message. See, he'd been a preacher, too, but was down on his luck when he lived here. I'm taking up the work where he had to leave off."

He moved around Sears, stepped into the crisp night air, and gleefully tasted the thrill of his encounter and the openmouthed stares of the saloon patrons at this revelation. Just maybe, out of sheer curiosity, they would come to the cabin. Joel did not care why they came, just so they did.

Responsibility downed his excitement. God had placed on him a heavy duty; he must not fail. Only through strict obedience to the Holy Spirit would the gospel's message touch and perhaps change Tomkinsville.

It did not take placards or banners to get the news out that a boy preacher had ridden into town, beat Eb Sears to the draw, invited him to ride for an Arizona cattle ranch, and would even hold a meeting the next Sunday. News ran like a spooked horse.

Tomkins said little but rounded up planks, hammer, and nails, and built some crude benches. "No telling how many folks will show up." His eyes twinkled. "Remember, I told folks you could preach as well as ride and rope and shoot." He pounded a few more nails, then eyed Joel. "I'd suggest you choose your sermon mighty careful," he added, but his eyes twinkled again.

Joel had already sensed the importance of this advice and soberly nodded his yellow head. When Tomkins refused help with his carpentering, Joel wandered off to a quiet knoll that offered as grand a view of the mountains as anything he had seen. What would appeal to the sturdy people of Tomkinsville? Certainly no watered-down message of a pallid Jesus. He closed his eyes and prayed for guidance. Warm sunlight surrounded him, and some of his feelings of inadequacy melted. Why should he fear? God had led him to this place; He would guide him.

Joel looked up at the craggy peaks above him. "I'd hate to get lost up there," he murmured, then sprang to his feet with an exultant yell. "That's it!" Thoughts raced through his brain. He pelted back to the cabin, past an astonished Tomkins. "I have my sermon," he called and bolted inside. He grabbed pencil, paper, and his worn Bible. By the time the benches stood sturdy and waiting, Joel's eyes shone and his heart thumped. "Thanks, God. This is just what's needed."

After the weeks on the trail, he felt a little strange when he donned his clean, pressed

39

suit on Sunday morning. The night before, he and Tomkins scoured the cabin to within an inch of its life and arranged the benches. They had no songbooks, but Joel possessed a clear, true voice and would line out hymns if his congregation did not know them. By the appointed time, every bench groaned under the weight of ranchers and their families, curious cowboys, townspeople, and round-eyed children who always looked forward to a circuit-riding preacher.

"What a friend we have in Jesus," the people enthusiastically sang. No need for Joel to sing a line and let them repeat. "All our sins and griefs to bear." He looked into their faces and saw the marks that sin had left in many, grief in others. His throat felt tight, and his vision blurred. What a tremendous need existed in Tomkinsville! The song ended. He offered a fervent prayer, and with one accord, the people said, "Amen." Then, Joel opened his Bible.

"Our text today is from Matthew 18, verses 12 and 13. 'How think ye? if a man have an hundred sheep, and one of them be gone astray, doth he not leave the ninety and nine, and goeth into the mountains, and seeketh that which is gone astray? And if so be that he find it, verily I say unto you, he rejoiceth more of that sheep, than of the ninety and nine which went not astray.' "

He closed the Bible. "Friends, we all know that sheepherders aren't too popular around these parts." Cattlemen and cowboys snickered. "Now, when Jesus told this story, He could have just as well talked about a cow critter or a good horse. I know if I had a hundred horses and Querida strayed, I'd tackle the roughest country around to find her." He glanced out the door, open to the warm autumn air, and pointed to the mountains. Heads turned and nodded. Joel caught a spark of interest in tired eyes.

"Our Lord doesn't tell how tough that journey was. Most of us have tackled rivers in flood, blizzards, or heat that would fry a lizard. Jesus doesn't say He had to fight off wolves or a mean old bear to save that sheep. He leaves out how steep the canyons were and the times when He maybe had to carry that sheep that was struggling to get away. Living here, you can imagine how it was."

The spark of interest flared into the flame of concentration. Joel rejoiced. "What the Lord does tell us is that if the sheep gets found and brought back home where it belongs, the owner is happier over it than over all the other ninety-nine that didn't go wandering off where they didn't belong."

He took a deep breath and stepped closer to his attentive listeners. "If any of you have ever had one of your children stray, you know just what the Lord means. You'd give your life in those mountains if that's what it took to bring back your child."

A subdued chorus of agreement rippled the air.

"Friends," Joel poignantly stretched out his hands, "that's just what God did. He sent His only Son, Jesus, so every one of us could be brought back from danger and have eternal life. He loved us that much. There's not a man, woman, or child here today who isn't being trailed by Jesus right now, just like that poor, lost sheep that strayed and was tracked, found, and delivered from hungry beasts and fierce storms. Unless we accept that and invite Him into our hearts and lives, why, we're worse off than that critter all alone and bleating somewhere in a dark canyon."

Joel paused, noted the wonderment in the children's faces, a mist in some of the women's eyes, the angry brushing away of a single drop on a cowboy's face. Too moved to say more, he simply said, "We will close by singing 'Praise God, from Whom All Blessings Flow.' "

The one sad note in the song and service

was Eb Sears's absence. Although Joel had not expected him, he had hoped. All through the hearty handshakes and exclamations of gladness that Joel had come, the young minister silently prayed for Sears.

When the congregation poured out, leading the stampede were the few sheepish-looking cowboys who had bashfully perched as close to the door as possible. Joel's keen ears caught a little byplay from among the cowboys that sent him posthaste after the others.

Fifty feet from the cabin, Eb Sears sat on a stocky bay that casually browsed near Querida and Tomkins's horse.

"Hey, Sears, you're too late for the preachin'," one of the cowboys sang out.

"Preachin'? Oh, yeah, there was a meetin', wasn't there?" Either Sears was the finest actor west of St. Louis, or he had forgotten. Joel suspected the first.

"Thought I'd see young Scott's black horse everyone's talkin' about," Sears explained elaborately and scratched his head, a devil-may-care expression on his face.

A few laughed, but no one challenged him, and Sears added, "What's her handle?"

"Querida. It means *beloved*. She's the first horse I ever saw foaled," Joel told the big

43

man, whose glistening eyes showed him to be a top judge of horseflesh.

"I reckon I rode out for nothin', huh. You're not goin' to sell her." The crowd lost interest and dispersed to buggies, wagons, and tethered horses.

Had Sears really come to see Querida? Joel did not think so. If he were a gambling man, he'd stake a lot that it had been the only way Sears would let himself get near a preacher, no matter how curious he might be. "No, I won't sell her, but I'm glad you came." For the second time, he shook hands with Sears, and the current that passed between them confirmed Joel's suspicions.

CHAPTER 3

If the gold aspens along the trails had whispered about Joel's encounter with Sears in the Missing Spur, now they sang his praises in a fluttering chorus. "Never heard a preacher preach like that" repeated itself over and over when ranchers or riders met. "That young feller talks about a God who knows Colorado and us simple folks. Never uses high-falutin' words, neither," a gnarled miner added.

Joel's second and third sermons merely added to his fame. So did the fun-loving, boyish spirit that led him into the impromptu races that Querida loved. But the test of his mettle came with the first snow.

Not everyone in Tomkinsville appreciated Joel's ministry. Business at the Missing Spur fell off when some of its patrons listened to the gospel and decided it was time to take a stand for the God who had done "a whole bunch" for them. Now, dark whispers joined

45

the praise. Tomkins reported a growing feeling, on the part of the faithful saloon crowd, against Joel's interfering in their business.

A few days later, he stamped in out of the cold, a worried look creasing his face. "Pardner, I hate like anything to tell you, but I've got to go back to Arizona."

"Really?" Joel raised astonished blue eyes from the sermon he had been preparing and looked at Tomkins. "Is something wrong?"

"My wife's back in Flagstaff," the older man explained. "We must have got our wires crossed. I thought she'd stay longer with her sister, but she's home and lonesome." He hesitated, and Joel saw the struggle going on within him.

"It's been good to come back, but —"

"You want to get home where you belong," Joel finished. He quietly added, "I understand. When do you want to leave?"

"There's a stage going out day after tomorrow."

The words hung in the cozy cabin. Joel saw regret in the way Tomkins looked yet eagerness over seeing his wife soon. "What about your horse?"

Tomkins shrugged. "You can have him. Take him with you, or better yet, sell him. He isn't my favorite. Now, if he were Querida, it would be another story." His keen gaze bored into Joel. "Do you still have plenty of money? Tomkinsville's been buzzing because you never take up an offering."

Joel flushed. "I don't need much. I'd rather the people would use their money to get a building for a church." He stretched. "I have a feeling I'll be riding on in the spring, but if there's some kind of building and folks are coming to services regularly, it shouldn't be too hard to get another preacher."

"Folks here don't want anyone but you," Tomkins said gruffly.

"I know, and it disturbs me," Joel admitted. "It's the Lord who needs to be praised, not me. Besides, I just can't help believing there's still a long trail ahead of me, and right now this is just a tarrying place." He shook with sudden melancholy. "I'll miss you, but if I had a wife back home . . ." His voice trailed off.

Tomkins climbed aboard the stage two days later but not before warning Joel, "Watch out for rattlers — the two-legged kind who don't have the courtesy to warn a man with their buzzing."

Joel agreed, then promptly forgot it. To his amazement, Eb Sears had dropped in to see him a time or two, although he never

47

came to the meetings. Joel still suspected Sears had heard every word of the first sermon but did not mention it, and the big man always had an excellent reason for stopping by. Once, it was to drop off a haunch of venison he said one of the ranchers had sent. The second time, he said he had heard that Joel wanted to sell Tomkins's horse. After a lot of bargaining, Sears paid a good price for it and laconically accepted Joel's offer for a cup of coffee.

"How come you're a preacher, anyhow?" he asked over the rim of his heavy mug. "Your ridin' and ropin' and the way ya handle a gun would get ya a job on any ranch."

Joel carefully blew on his coffee to gain time to know what to tell him. Then, to his own amazement, he found himself telling his whole story to Sears, who let his coffee grow cold and grunted now and then. "So your own daddy shoved off the blame on his brother," he finally exclaimed. "Still, ya want to find him?"

A longing, greater than ever before, rose in Joel. "I have to. The note I mentioned where he asked to be forgiven shows he isn't, maybe wasn't, all bad." A somber mood crept into the little cabin; he shook it off. "Maybe, because I never knew a real

48

father, my aunt Judith's teachings about my heavenly Father meant more. God also helped me not to be bitter, just sorry. Someday, if I can find my own father and tell him that, maybe he will contact his own parents before it's too late. It would mean the world to them. It would mean even more if he could find and accept God's forgiveness."

Sears abruptly stood. "You're all right, Kid. Just keep on tellin' folks about that God of yours." He strode to the door. "It's kinda comfortin' to think that He's trailin' after even worn-out cowpokes like me. Maybe someday I — some of us'll stop ridin' long enough to let Him catch up." The door banged behind Sears, but a flood of light and joy poured into Joel's soul.

It proved short lived. The next night, gunshots outside Joel's cabin sent him pell-mell into the night. The clatter of hooves sounded loud in his ears, then dwindled toward town. A light snow under a lopsided moon showed Querida tossing her head and dancing away from a huddled dark heap that stirred, moaned, then lay silent.

"God, what's happened?" Joel snatched the horse's reins, wondering how she had gotten loose and berating himself for not building a locked shelter for her sooner. He flipped the reins over a low-hanging tree branch and dropped to his knees beside the crumpled figure. Heavy breathing showed life, and Joel turned the body face up toward the moonlight. "Sears!" He ran his hand inside the unconscious man's jacket. His fingers came away warm with the sickening feel and smell of blood.

Every ounce of range-trained muscle and sinew worked together in a mighty burst of strength that got the far-heavier man onto Joel's shoulders and into the cabin. He staggered across the floor. Blood dripped down Sears's arm and left a ghastly red trail behind them. Once, Sears opened his eyes, but he did not speak. Then he lapsed into merciful oblivion.

Joel grabbed a knife and slit Sears's jacket. His stomach lurched when he pulled jacket and shirt open and exposed a smooth back that spurted blood. "Bullet must have gone in the front and come out here." He left Sears long enough to jerk a clean towel from a nail, fold it, and shove it against the wound with one hand. The other hand fumbled with Sears's neckerchief and pressed it against the man's chest where the bullet had entered. The towel soaked through. Joel wadded up the jacket and used it.

"God, I have to have help, or he will die. What shall I do?" He looked despairingly at the door. "If I leave him, he'll bleed to death. Please, send help!"

A minute or an eternity later, hoofbeats, then a call, "Preacher, you all right?" rang like heavenly music in Joel's ears. Two men, solid citizens who had openly proclaimed the need for a preacher in their town, burst through the still-open door. "We heard shots," one said as the second pushed past. "What's goin' on here?"

"Ride for the doctor," Joel sharply ordered. The first man bolted, and rapid hoofbeats sent thankfulness through the young preacher. "Hand me another towel. I can't get the blood stopped," Joel told the second man. Strong hands instantly snatched a towel, wadded it, and he said, "Let me." He held it ready until Joel slid his hands out of the way, then he pressed steadily. By the time the messenger returned with the doctor, the worst of the flow had been staunched.

"Looks like you've been butcherin' hogs in here," the doctor commented. "Get me hot water, clean rags." His dour face and matter-of-fact orders strangely comforted Joel. Obviously, gunshot wounds were a large part of the doctor's practice. He

51

stitched and cleansed and bandaged but shook his head. "I don't recommend moving him far. Are you willing to keep him here? He's lost a lot of blood." The doctor looked dubious, and Joel's hopes fell again.

"He stays here." Joel motioned to Tomkins's room, then went in to make up the bed. "And he's going to make it." He folded his lips in a way that stopped possible argument, and thus began the long fight for Eb Sears's life.

It took all of Joel's prayers and the doctor's skills. For days, death lurked on the cabin's doorstep, grinning, waiting for its prey. Yet, Eb Sears's dogged determination coupled with the care he received, and he slowly began to mend.

Joel and the doctor had long since pieced together the story of the fateful night in the snow. Sears's delirium had loosed his tongue and revealed the heroism he would never have admitted to under normal circumstances. Sears had discovered a plot to murder "that interferin' kid preacher" and make it look like he had been shot during the rustling of Querida. Everyone knew of Joel's love for his horse. Nothing would be more natural than his rushing out to save the mare and being shot in the confusion.

Hoping to warn Joel, Sears sneaked out to

the cabin but had arrived too late and evidently had been mistaken for the victim. Not even he knew exactly who was in on the nefarious scheme, but Tomkinsville noted the significance of certain Missing Spur habitués who mysteriously disappeared in the night. A posse rode out, but enough snow had fallen to cover tracks, and they turned back.

Joel marveled at the strange paths God used to accomplish His work. Years earlier, Sears had been felled by a jealous man who had hoped to get rid of two enemies at once. Now, he had saved Joel's life by nearly giving his own. In addition, the devotion Joel showed in his care for Sears won for him even higher esteem than all of his preaching.

A greater good came from it. The people of Tomkinsville rose in their might and declared that either the Missing Spur tone down or the town would be missing a saloon. The worried proprietor, who might or might not have been part of the plot, instituted some rules and shortened the hours the saloon stayed open. An "accidental" shooting of someone was one thing, but the deliberate planning of a murder and the resultant near killing of Sears did more to clean up the wild atmosphere of the town than Joel had even dreamed of.

Not until it was safe to leave Sears in willing, protective hands did Joel hold church again, this time in the lobby of the town's hotel. It was packed, and at the end of the service, a leading citizen announced that people were contributing money and that as soon as the weather cooperated — which might not be until spring — Tomkinsville would have its own church. He added, "With all due respect, I reckon seeing you live out what you preached and watching you take care of Eb Sears has showed us what we need to do." Joel had to bite his lip to keep from letting out a cowboy yell of happiness.

A few days later, Joel returned home to a table groaning with home-canned goods, two dressed chickens, and a bushel basket of root vegetables. "What's all this?"

Eb grinned, the first real smile Joel had seen on him since the shooting. "Folks musta thought I needed more n'r'shment than I was gettin'. They brought this over." He squirmed and winced.

"When's the boys gonna bring a wagon and haul me outa here?" His face turned dull red. "I've been clutterin' up your cabin long enough."

A wild idea popped into Joel's head and out his mouth. "Why don't you stick around, spend the winter here with me? It's lonesome since Tomkins left." He saw a wistfulness in the other man's face, quickly hidden, and blandly went on. "No one's going to be out rounding up cattle until spring, anyway."

Eb opened his mouth to speak, but Joel forestalled him. "Soon as you feel like it, there's lots you could do. I'd like to go hunting but don't know the country. Then with winter about to pounce on us, we'll need a mountain of wood."

"I'll think on it. Not sure how I'd like livin' with a preacher, even one who ain't like any preacher I ever met."

Joel wisely kept silent. Sears must have thought on it, but the subject never came up again. The minute the doctor pronounced him fit to ride, however, he took Joel on a hunting trip that ended with enough venison to provide them meat for a long time.

During the weeks together, Sears became "Eb" and "Preacher" changed to "Joel." A bond forged between the two men, and Joel learned the other side of the grudge that had caused the problem between Gideon

55

and Sears.

"Only girl I ever cottoned to," Eb said one evening when the fire roared in the fireplace and shadows hid his face. "She liked me, too, until your uncle came. I knew I wasn't good enough for her, but I never meant bad by her." He shifted uneasily and stared into the flames. "I was aimin' to ask her to marry me, so I got sore when Gideon — Cyrus then — sent her out of town. I got drunk, which I hadn't done for a long time, made some dirty comments, and got showed up in front of everyone." He sighed. "Wonder what happened to Lily? Some lucky hand prob'ly lassoed her."

"In the spring, I'm going to Colorado Springs," Joel said quietly, aware of what it had cost this private man to share his feelings. "Gideon wanted me to especially look you up — and Lily."

Eb's big frame jerked. "Whaat?"

"That's right. He feels he missed the chance to tell you about God and won't ever be really happy until he knows you've heard it. Lily, too."

Eb's breathing quickened. "Sometimes I get tired of Tomkinsville." He leaned forward and poked at the fire, keeping his face carefully averted. "Since you're goin' to Colorado Springs, maybe I'll ride along.

56

Not to see Lily, or anythin'," he hastily added. "When you're ridin' a horse like Querida, a feller can't be too careful."

Joel hid the twitch of his lips, but his eyes brimmed with laughter. "I'd be glad to have you. Oh, if you ever get tired enough of Tomkinsville to leave, I think you'd really like Arizona."

In the spring of 1889, over the protests of the majority of Tomkinsville, Joel and Eb Sears rode away, promising to see if a minister could be found for the little church that would be built soon. They silently halted Querida and the stocky bay that Eb rode. "Ranger's a good horse," he said, and pride shone in his eyes. "Not rustler bait like your Querida, but a good horse." He had sold the horse he bought from Joel to pay his way to Colorado Springs and to get some new clothes. "Never thought I'd wish I saved my money." He laughed, then turned the corners of his mouth down. "I guess it ain't too late. If I should take a notion to go see the Double J ranch of yours in Arizony, I don't wanta ride in lookin' like some scarecrow. Your folks'd think you took up with low comp'ny."

"They'll never think that about you, Eb," Joel said.

Admiration that had begun with the older man's willing sacrifice to save Joel and had grown during the winter months brought an unaccustomed gentleness to Eb's face, but all he said was, "Adiós, Tomkinsville. Maybe I'll see ya again and maybe I won't." He waved to the town in the valley, then rode down the trail, giving Joel a moment alone to silently bid farewell to his first parish and to offer a special prayer that the work the Lord had allowed him to begin might continue in this tiny part of the country.

The closer they got to Colorado Springs, the quieter Sears grew. Finally, Joel demanded, "Eb, something's been eating you ever since we rode out of Tomkinsville. What is it?"

A sigh came clear from the rundown heels of Sears's boots. His face filled with misery. "What if we can't find Lily? It's been a lotta years. Or worse, what if we find her and she —" He choked on the words.

Sympathy and wonder at a love that could live for such a long time without nourishment roughened Joel's voice. "We'll find her, and she'll be the same girl you knew except now she'll be a woman — nearly thirty."

"I hope so." Sears's gloomy countenance did not lighten. "Sometimes I think I oughta stayed back there." He jerked a thumb toward the west. "Fool thing. Here I am gettin' close to forty and chasin' over the countryside like a moonstruck calf."

"Who says age has anything to do with love?" Joel flared back. "Wait 'til you get to the Double J and see Judith and Gideon. They're more in love now than when they got back together in Arizona, and that's been almost as many years since you saw Lily." He pressed his point home. "Not many men are privileged to love someone the way you've done. Honestly, even though things didn't work out the way you wanted them to, would you trade your feelings and memories?"

"Not for a gold mine." Sears's eyes flashed, then he grinned shamefacedly.

Joel threw back his head, and a clear, ringing laugh brought a reluctant smile to his partner's lips. Then Eb said, "Just ya wait. One of these days some purty little filly's gonna get ya standin' on your head, then I'll be the one to haw-haw." Anticipation stamped a boyish look on his features. "Ya still ain't said how we'll find Lily."

"Don't you think that if God brought me hundreds of miles to make sure she knows about Him, He can help us find her?"

Sears cocked his head to one side. "I don't see no signposts nailed on trees and sayin', 'This way to Lily.'" A crooked grin replaced his grumbling. "But, we ain't there yet."

Joel laughed again, but a frown puckered his forehead. He gazed unseeingly down the well-traveled road they had found when they left the trail. "I wish I could be as sure of finding my father as I am of finding Lily. Eb, if Lily's married and happy, would you consider going on to Texas with me, at least for a spell? We got along over the winter." Desire for human companionship on his uncertain journey crept into his voice.

Sears grunted. "Maybe. Watch out there, Ranger!" He swerved the bay to the side of the road to make room for a wagon coming toward them. Querida followed.

"How far to town?" Joel called when the nondescript wagon pulled abreast of them.

"Less than a mile." The driver waved and drove on.

Joel felt the stiffening go out of his knees. He had blithely promised to find Lily. *God, please help us.* Such a few words to request aid. *If only everyone realized how available God is!*

It took time, in a town as big as Colorado

60

Springs, to find anyone who might know Lily. Joel and Eb inquired at a couple of rooming houses, some stores, and a bank. Always the answer was, "No, don't recall a Lily." Many of those they questioned were recent arrivals.

"Try the stage line," one helpful man advised. But the old-time drivers had long since moved on, replaced by young fellows.

For five days they searched in vain, then Joel came down to breakfast in the modest lodgings they had found and announced, "We've been going at it all wrong."

"Who sez?" Sears put down a forkful of flapjacks dripping syrup.

"What we need to do is find out who the old-timers are around here." Joel attacked the steaming plate of cakes their landlady slid before him. "We'll go back to the biggest dry goods store and start there." Eb eyed him but said nothing. Thirty minutes later, they marched into the emporium. "Who's the owner?" Joel asked a clerk.

"Why, Mr. Livingston." The pale-faced young man in a store-bought suit looked surprised. "His office is up there." He waved toward a set of stairs. "Go right up."

Conscious of the clerk's stares, Joel grinned and told Eb, "Soon as we find where she is, we'll get you a suit like that

61

jasper's wearing."

Eb just snorted and kept on climbing.

Five minutes later, a secretary, who could be a twin to the clerk, ushered them into Livingston's office. A sigh of relief escaped Joel. Good. The gray-haired man looked old enough to have settled Colorado Springs, but even thick glasses failed to hide his keen eyes.

"Sir, we're looking for a girl who came in on the stage from a mining town named Tomkinsville about thirteen years ago," Joel began. "Her name is Lily."

The man sprang from his chair; his glasses fell to the floor and shattered. "Lily! Who are you, and what do you want with her?" His hands shook, and he stared at the strangers.

A great leap of hope warmed Joel's words. "Years ago, my uncle helped her get here. My name is Joel Scott, and this is Eb Sears who used to know Lily."

Unashamed tears stood in Livingston's eyes. "Thank God you've come. If ever Lily needed friends, it's now."

Sears pushed past Joel and confronted the distraught man. His big hands worked. "Where is she?" he demanded hoarsely. "What are ya to her, and why is she needin' friends so bad?"

62

Livingston fumbled in his pocket and brought out another pair of glasses. He slipped them on, obviously fighting for control. "Lily is my daughter-in-law. I gave her work when she first came to town. My son fell in love with her, and they married. Last fall he was thrown and killed. Since then, Lily's changed from a happy woman to a little black shadow. Doctors say it's shock and if she doesn't come out of it soon, she'll die."

CHAPTER 4

"No!" Eb gave a strangled cry, then determination straightened his shoulders and snapped his head into a fighting position. Color came back to his pale face, and he wordlessly turned to Joel.

"May we see her?" Joel hesitated. "Or would it be better if you told her we were here and asked if she'd see us?"

Livingston shook his head. "She's refused to see anyone except my wife and me and the boy."

"Boy?"

"My grandson. He's five, only child she and my son could have. I think if it hadn't been for him, she'd have given up before this. But she's so tired from refusing to eat, even for Danny's sake, she can't go on much longer. Perhaps the surprise of seeing you will bring her around." He turned to Eb and held out his hands imploringly. "Forgive me for asking, but did you care for her?"

"From the first time I saw her." It came from the heart.

"Thank God." Livingston wrung Sears's hand. "Come with me."

Eb looked down at his riding garb. "Shouldn't I get some better clothes? I aimed to buy a suit."

"No, no." Livingston impatiently shook his head. He led his visitors out a private entrance, down a flight of stairs to the street, and across it. "Be what she remembers."

Joel and Eb silently followed the almost-running store owner a few blocks over to a residential area. A large, white frame house sat back in a cluster of trees. Livingston threw open the door and ushered them inside. A sweet-faced older woman rose from a low chair, her hands dripping yarn and bright knitting needles. A dark-haired, dark-eyed child solemnly looked up from his place on the floor at his grandmother's feet. Joel heard Eb's quick intake of breath and knew Danny must be the childish reflection of Lily.

"Mama, this is Eb Sears, an old friend of Lily's," Livingston explained. "The young man is Joel Scott, nephew of the kind young stranger who gave her money and sent her to Colorado Springs."

65

Emotion crumpled the woman's face, and she hastily said, "Danny, go to the kitchen, and ask Hannah to give you a cookie."

"All right, Grandma." The child trotted away.

For a moment, Joel became that child, being sent away while grown-ups talked. He remembered the brown faces of the Mexican servants at the Circle S and how Rosa and Carmelita welcomed a tired, uncertain little boy.

Then, Livingston said, "I'll just take Mr. Sears up first, if it's all right." He looked anxiously from Eb to Joel. "Lily won't know you, Mr. Scott."

"That's fine," Joel said, but he leaned close to Sears and whispered in his ear, "I'll be praying."

Eb gripped his hand. "Come as far as the door in case I need ya." Joel quietly followed the other two men up a flight of stairs, down a comfortable hall to an open door, then stopped. Livingston stepped through with Sears right behind.

"Lily, here's an old friend, come all the way from Tomkinsville to see you."

Joel could see every detail of the airy, wallpapered room and the slender, girlish woman who slowly rose from a rocking chair. Her dark eyes all but filled her thin

66

face. Seldom had he encountered such gulfs of despair and sadness. *God, give Eb the right words.*

"Howdy, Lily." In the strain of the moment, all Sears's insouciance rose to sustain him. "You've been under the weather, huh?" He crossed the room with his hand held out.

She stumbled toward him. "Eb? Eb Sears?" A flicker of life stole into her eyes. "Why, after all these years! You look just the same."

"You don't," he told her frankly. "You're better lookin' now than ya were in Tomkinsville." A blush stained her pearly face, but Eb took her little white hands in his for a moment, then released them. "Sorry about your husband, Lily, but ya sure have a great little buckaroo downstairs. He's a mite puny, though. Now that spring's here, you'll need to be gettin' him out in the fresh air so he can get some color."

Joel had caught the flash of pain when Eb mentioned Lily's husband, but it disappeared into a little frown at the word *puny.* How wise of Eb to get her attention on her son and off her own problems. Concern for Danny could be the first step to her own healing.

"I brought someone you'll wanta see," Eb continued. "Joel Scott, nephew to the Scott

67

who rode in, staked Tomkins, and sent ya out of Tomkinsville." He stepped aside, and Joel came into the pretty room.

"Lily, my uncle Gideon — who called himself Cyrus when he knew you — never forgot you or Eb." Joel quietly explained how Gideon could no longer travel long distances without pain and that he had come in Gideon's place. The growing interest in her face rewarded him. "Most of all, he wanted to tell you how much he regretted failing you."

"Failing me!" Lily backed away and sat back down in her rocker. "Cy— Gideon Scott *saved* me. If it hadn't been for him, I'd never have come here or met Dan or had little Danny or . . ." Her hands tightened on the arms of her chair.

Joel nodded, pleased with her response but noting how tired she looked. "Gideon sent you a special message, but it can wait. You need to rest. We'll come back later if you like." He held his breath.

"For supper, perhaps?" Lily looked at her father-in-law, who eagerly agreed. The three men walked out and back downstairs. Mrs. Livingston stood waiting.

"Mama, she's coming down for supper, and these men will be our guests." Happy tears filled the woman's eyes and overflowed when Livingston brokenly explained, "It will be the first time in more than a month that Lily has left her room." In a wave of thanks and more tears, Eb and Joel finally got away, promising to be back no later than five o'clock.

With one accord, they walked to the livery stable, saddled and mounted Querida and Ranger, and rode for miles, viewing Colorado Springs and the surrounding area.

When they headed back to town, Sears quietly said, "I'm still goin' to get new clothes, but no dud's trappin's. Lily ain't used to me in city clothes." He paused and waited until they reached the stable again before adding, "Joel, ya may have to go lookin' for your daddy without me." His rock-stern expression softened, and he glanced in the direction of the Livingston home. "Somehow, this feels like the end of the trail for this cowpoke. I ain't askin' anythin' of Lily 'cept to be a friend. I just feel I can help her and the buckaroo by stickin' around."

"I understand," Joel assured his friend. "The Double J will always be there no matter what happens."

"Yeah." Eb cleared his throat. "Uh, when ya said that God of yours would help us, I was leery. But we found her, didn't we?" He took a deep breath, held it, then expelled it. "If He makes her well, I'll start ridin' His trail."

"No, *no,* Eb!"

Joel's outcry froze Sears. His face hardened. "Ain't I good enough, after all ya said about Him followin' lost critters?" He laughed bitterly. "Mighta known I was playin' against a stacked deck."

"It's not that." Joel felt compelled as he had never been before. His heart burned. "Everything I said is true, but you can't bargain with God the way you'd horse trade, promising Him this if He'll do that. You know I'd give anything for you to follow the Master, but it has to be everything or nothing. Either you choose to do what you know is right and stick with it *even if Lily dies,* or it's no good, Eb."

The anger faded from Sears's face. A muscle in his left cheek twitched. "That's a mighty powerful prop'sition," he said slowly.

"It can't be any other way. Otherwise, the only reason we'd accept Christ would be for what we could get out of it."

"Isn't that what a feller does anyway?" Sears demanded. "He says yes to God so he can skitter out of gettin' punished for all the mean things he's done."

Joel never wavered. "Some folks do just

that, but people who are smart give themselves because they love and appreciate what God did for them, not just to keep from getting what they deserve."

Eb grunted and changed the subject. Joel, however, noticed how thoughtful and withdrawn Eb acted while selecting his new shirt, vest, boots, hat, and pants at the emporium and while shaving, more carefully than usual. At five minutes to five, they knocked on the Livingstons' door, shiny-clean and expectant. A new dignity surrounded Sears, and Joel realized that the selflessness evident in his friend's life had changed a tough rider into a man who would put aside his own desires for the sake of another.

By early summer, Lily had lost much of the shadow in her eyes. Eb simply would not allow her to remain in her room and brood. Time after time, he coaxed her into walking, then riding, "Because Danny needs his mama, not just a roughneck like me," as he said.

Sometimes Joel joined them. He had faithfully delivered Gideon's message, the gospel of salvation, to Lily. In her, he found depths of bitterness that God would allow the husband she had loved to die in a senseless

71

accident. Yet, Lily found gradual healing in the fact that God had lost His only Son — not in an accident, but in the deliberate plan to save His creation. She began to open like a tightly closed rosebud, and by the time Joel rode away in late summer, Lily and Eb both hovered on the edge of committing their lives to their Master.

Joel had intended to follow the trail to Wyoming and Montana that Gideon had taken, but the inner urgency that had prodded him, then subsided, rose sharply. On a clear summer morning, he shook hands with Sears, vaulted onto Querida's back, and turned his face toward Texas.

Well past nineteen, he no longer looked all boy. New maturity firmed his lips except when he smiled. The experiences of the past months showed in his compassionate gaze, a gaze that held more tolerance for those who slipped and fell than when he first left Arizona. Where once he would have condemned, now he stooped to lift. Yet, always in the depths of his heart, fire and ice lived side by side: the fire of his passion to find Cyrus Scott, the icy realization it might never come to pass. The thought made him tremble, and the long miles Querida carried him became hours for introspection. He had never been alone for such an extended time.

First Tomkins, then Sears had provided an older and more experienced influence. Now he rode alone except for the uncanny feeling of companionship he knew must be God.

At times, Joel and Querida were tiny black dots, the only moving creatures in a vast expanse of sky and land. Then it was that Joel missed the mountains, the wilderness. How could anyone live forever in a rolling country that stretched from horizon to horizon in every direction with never having the friendly peak of a jutting mountain to offer encouragement? In sheer desperation, he sought out those riding his way, often veering from his course for the sake of hearing another human voice. After a few times, he gave this up; the naked greed in the eyes of many who he met betrayed their lust for Querida, and he slipped away.

Tired and drooping, Joel trailed into San Scipio country. He was amazed at how much he recognized and was thrilled when landmarks brought the familiar feeling he had been there before.

Almost a year after he left the Double J, the young minister and his faithful Querida, more beloved than ever after their arduous journey, *clip-clopped* into the dusty town that had changed so little that Joel blinked

73

in astonishment. Had San Scipio been asleep these long years? No, for on closer examination, he saw signs of weathering, a few new houses. Yet, the illusion of time standing still persisted, so much so that he gasped in astonishment when he saw the church his grandfather had built now had a small, cozy cabin next to it with smoke curling from the chimney.

Tempted to stop and see who lived there, Joel shook his head. "Not yet," he told Querida. "Just a little longer, and we'll be at the Circle S." Strange that he had not said home, or was it? Most of his life had been on the Double J. "Trot along, Querida. Maybe there will be letters from home."

In response to his voice, the black mare raised her drooping head, pricked her ears, and speeded up while Joel's keen gaze shifted from side to side in his unwillingness to miss any cherished childhood sites. Then they topped the promontory rise that overlooked the Circle S; below lay the ranch, warmed by the late afternoon sun. With a cry, Joel slid from the saddle. He raised his glance to the hills and felt a surge of strength go through him. Surely God would somehow, in some way, lead him to his father. Why else would he feel closer to that unknown man than at any other time in his life?

Stiff from long hours riding, Joel swung back into his saddle and started down to the valley. With every step Querida took, Joel relived childhood days on the Circle S. The cottonwoods he had climbed now rose tall with many years' growth. But the house looked the same — foot-thick cream walls that held heat in or cold out, depending on the season. A red-tiled roof that glistened in the sun. Joel's heart pumped. He had not sent word of his arrival, and mischief tilted his mouth skyward. He would just bet that Grandpa and Grandma would be surprised at how much he had changed from the almost seven-year-old who rode away atop a covered wagon. Yet, when he reached the hacienda-style house and called, "Anyone home?" Joel knew the seven-year-old boy still lived inside him.

The massive front door opened, and a man stepped out. Life's tragedies had silvered his hair, thinned him to gauntness, and carved permanent furrows in his face. But they had not been able to bow the large head or bend the shoulders that were held as erect as Joel remembered. Intent on the similarities and changes in Lige, Joel stayed in the saddle until the booming voice he would have recognized anywhere asked,

"Well, are you going to sit there all day? Light down, Boy." In three giant strides, Lige reached Querida and held out his hand. His ox eyes rolled, still blue as Texas bluebonnets.

Joel dismounted, grabbed the large hand, and felt his eyes sting. He opened his mouth to speak, but a rush of flying feet halted him. A whirlwind with wiry arms and a tear-stained face caught him. "My baby!"

"Don't carry on, Naomi," Lige told his laughing, crying wife. "Let him loose long enough to look at him. He's no baby."

Joel's grandmother pulled back. Although her hair had also whitened, she looked less changed than Lige. Her eyes still snapped in the way he remembered. "Elijah Scott, it doesn't matter if he is half as tall as a mountain, this is my little boy come home." She hugged him again, announced, "Your room is ready," and fled toward the front door. "By the time you're washed up, Rosa and Carmelita will have a meal ready. You look like you could use one! There'll be hot water in your room. See that you use it. I never saw such a dusty rider." She vanished inside after her pronouncements from the porch.

"I guess Grandma will never believe I'm grown up." Joel laughed. The peppery nature that hid beneath her usual calm made him a child again. Strangely, it felt good.

"Mighty fine piece of horseflesh." Lige turned from Joel to the tired mare. "This the one you wrote about when you were a lad?"

"Yes." Joel caught the reins in one hand and headed for the corral. "I need to clean her up. She's carried me a long way."

"Better not risk Naomi's wrath," Lige suggested with the hint of a twinkle in his eyes. "I'll care for — what's her name?"

"Querida — Spanish for *beloved*."

Lige looked amused but did not say anything, just took the reins and admonished, "I'd step lively, if I were you."

Joel did. He barely wasted a glance on the large hall except to see it had not changed. The polished dark floor and furniture attested to loving care. Bright serapes on the cream plaster walls and matching, woven Mexican rugs welcomed him. So did the courtyard just outside, abloom with late summer flowers. The fountain splashed just the same as the fateful day he and Judith came to the Circle S. He started toward the large room and alcove they had used while there.

"Not there." Naomi appeared at his elbow.

"You'll have Gideon's rooms." Her voice sounded choked. "You are so like him — and your father." The hand she laid on his arm trembled, but the next moment she dashed it across her eyes and crisply reminded him to hurry.

After his long journey from Colorado, Joel found himself content to mosey around the ranch, let Querida rest, and simply soak up the outward peace of the Circle S. Still, after a few days, his youthful resilience overcame his fatigue, and he spent hours riding with Lige. He received a visit from the San Scipio minister, a frank-faced, likable fellow who lived in the little cabin next to the church with his wife and baby.

"I'd be proud to have you preach come Sunday," the minister invited.

Joel hesitated, then caught the perceptible nod from his grandmother and Lige's quickly smothered grin. "I'd be happy to accept," he agreed.

After the visitor drove away, Joel asked, "Do they — the church — know it wasn't Gideon —" He could not go on in the face of the pain that replaced Lige's half smile and his gruff, "They know," before the big man stood and walked out.

"I had to ask." Joel stared at his hands.

78

"I know, Dear." His grandmother twisted her apron, then smoothed out the folds with painstaking care; Joel's heart twisted at the action. "I don't know how much you remember of that time or what Judith told you, but the Sunday after the message came from Cyrus asking forgiveness, Lige went to church alone. He wouldn't even let me accompany him. Later I learned that he courteously waited until after the sermon had ended, then told the church how unjust he had been to his younger son because of his blind love of the older. He has never mentioned his confession, but I know it must have cruelly knifed his pride." Her hands stilled, and a poignant blue light shone in her eyes. "Joel, there is no man bigger than one who will publicly admit he's wrong, even when the cost is high."

A wave of love and admiration for his grandfather tightened Joel's throat and made his heart pound. He blurted out sympathy and went to find Lige. Before the matter could be closed forever, he must again rush in where wise men would not.

He found Lige standing with one arm resting on the corral fence while he gazed toward the distant mountains. Without turning, he said, "She told you."

"Yes." Joel inhaled a blend of stable and

hay odors. He wanted to cry out his feelings, but Lige had moved to some remote, unapproachable place. Joel's stubbornness rose. "Not many men would do what you did." If he lived as many years as some Old Testament patriarchs, he would never forget Lige Scott's reply.

His grandfather whipped toward him, eyes blazing with sapphire fire. "Boy, any *man* would." Lige strode away, looking even taller to Joel than ever before.

Saturday night at supper, Joel fired the first gun in a private campaign. "Why don't you sell the Circle S and move to Arizona? Gideon can't do all the riding and overseeing of the ranch he'd like to. He sure could use another good hand." He shot a covert glance at Lige and blandly continued, "Grandma, Aunt Judy really needs help with the twins." He chuckled. "Matt and Millie were eight when I left and perfect rascals. I don't know what they're like now, but they're bound to need a firm hand."

"Leave Texas?" Lige's heavy eyebrows met in a forbidding line. "Never!"

"Now, Lige," Naomi began, wistfulness at the mention of the twins softening her face. "My heart's plain hungry to see Gideon and the rest."

Lige shook his massive head as if she had

hit him with a log. "You want to sell this place we've worked to build and go kiting off to Arizona? Woman, are you out of your mind?"

"No." She helped herself to more chili and passed the enormous bowl to Joel. "I just want to see my son." A spasm of pain contorted her smooth face. "We've waited here all these years hoping Cyrus would come back. He hasn't. Must I die without seeing either boy again?"

All the fight went out of Lige. He paled and, for the first time, looked old to Joel, shrunken.

"I don't mean you should sell immediately," he quickly put in. "Why don't you go to Flagstaff for a visit? See how you like the country? Your foreman's run the Circle S for years and can handle things while you're gone."

Lige straightened, and interest crept into his face. "Would you stay here while we're gone — if we go?"

A sickening flood of anguish filled Joel. How could he tell — but he had to say it. "Grandpa, I can't. Ever since I left the Double J, I've felt God had a special mission for me. That's why I'm here, as well as to see you."

Recognition, shock, hope flared in Lige's

81

eyes. "And this mission is —"

Joel licked dry lips. His hands felt cold, his face hot. "To find my . . . my father."

Lige sucked in his breath. Naomi gave a little cry.

Joel leaned forward and planted his hands on the tablecloth before him. "I hope you'll go. There's been too many years between you and my Arizona family." His hands clenched. "Even if you stay, I'll be riding out right after I preach on Sunday."

CHAPTER 5

"Who am I?"

Rebecca Fairfax despairingly stretched her arms out toward the panorama before her, searching for secrets the distant wilderness might hold. How many times had she ridden to this eastern New Mexico vista in hopes it would trigger memories that tumbled in her mind, too ephemeral to hold? Some, Kit Carson and Lucien Maxwell among them, said the scene that lay before her was the grandest in New Mexico. The fan-shaped holdings of the Lazy F ranch lay between forested slopes and rolling plains where the Old Santa Fe Trail and Cimarron River wound into the blue distance. Thousands of acres, broken by a few cattle ranches, spread west past slopes that jutted sharply to glistening, white-peaked mountains. How she loved them! If only —

"Thought I'd find you here."

Vermilion, the mustang that Smokey Travis had broken and given to the girl on her eighteenth birthday just a few months before in December, shied and danced away from the man on foot who had sneaked up on them. Rebecca expertly quieted him, then turned. "What are you doing, creeping up on me, Hayes?" Her usually merry brown eyes flashed fire. Rebellious tendrils of her nut-brown hair had escaped her sombrero and curled moistly around her flushed, angry face. "I told you before to leave me alone!"

Admiration for her charm lightened Clyde Hayes's heavy, sullen face. Bold gray eyes surveyed her from dusty boot tops up her lithe, five-foot, six-inch frame. Hayes doffed his worn Stetson, exposing mousy brown hair. "It's time we had a talk," he announced.

Ugh, how I hate him, she thought. In the last year, he had turned the ranch from a place of freedom to a nightmare. Well, she would not stand for it. "I have nothing to say to you," she retorted.

"Fine way for a woman to talk about the man she's goin' to marry." Triumph leered in his eyes. "Your daddy promised you to me five years ago when I took over as foreman."

Sheer rage threatened to topple Rebecca

from the saddle where she could stick like a cactus on the wildest horse. "Marry you?" She laughed scornfully and rejoiced when an ugly red crept into Hayes's face. "You're thirty-five years old, almost old enough to be my father. Even if you weren't, do you think I'd marry a man I hate with all my heart, especially since you tried to maul me coming home from the rodeo in Raton last fall?"

The red deepened. "Aw, Becky, you know I'd been drinkin' and —"

"And didn't have the decency of a rabid skunk." She dug her spurless boot heels into Vermilion's sides. He snorted, leaped, and Hayes jumped aside, but not before the stallion's shoulder caught him with a glancing blow and sent the would-be suitor flying.

Rebecca laughed again and called back over her shoulder, "Next time I'll run you down. Stay out of our way, Hayes." As soon as they reached level land, she goaded Vermilion into a dead run. Even if Hayes were mounted, he could not catch her. Not a horse for a hundred miles around equaled Vermilion.

Wind whistled past her, and if the girl's sombrero had not been firmly mashed down on her head, the hat would have gone sailing. Her laughter changed to joy, and her spirits rose, but by the time she reached the Lazy F, they drooped again. *Has Father really promised me to Hayes? If so, why?* As clearly as if it had been this morning, she remembered the day the two-hundred-pound man came. Even at thirteen, she had instinctively distrusted him, and she avoided him all she could. Perhaps the change in her father troubled her most. From the moment Hayes took over, Samuel Fairfax lost even the small amount of patience with her that he had shown before.

Now Rebecca wondered, *Does Hayes know something that would discredit Father? If not, why did he lord it over the hands until, one by one, he drove them away?*

Smokey Travis was the exception. Twenty-one, only a few inches taller than Rebecca, he had stuck. Without being vain, she knew the reason — herself. A little smile added sweetness to her lips. She did not mind having Smokey in love with her. It had changed the harum-scarum cowboy from a gambling, drinking man who kept up with the best — no, the worst — of the riders to a considerate, thoughtful protector.

Dark-haired, dark-eyed, and droll, Smokey refused to let Hayes drive him away, and when he could do so without raising Hayes's ire and ending up fired after three years of top service, Smokey unobtrusively saved the girl from encounters with the persistent foreman.

Sometimes Rebecca considered eloping with Smokey. He had never suggested it, but the way his midnight gaze followed her spoke eloquently. If she married him, she would have love and respect, not what she sensed in Hayes — his desire to possess and tame her the way she had seen him tame a wild horse.

"I'm glad he didn't get you," she whispered to Vermilion. The red stallion whinnied. "Smokey used kindness, not mastery. I wonder if real mastery actually is kindness?" She stroked Vermilion's glistening shoulder, uncoiled the lariat she always carried on her saddlehorn, and swung it in a wide loop. It dropped over the gatepost to the corral. Still in the saddle, Rebecca gave an expert tug, and the gate swung open.

"Good girl." The sound of applause from the rider perched on the fence changed her mood again. Smokey Travis's teeth gleamed white against his deeply tanned skin. His dark eyes sparkled. "Where'd you ride? I finished my chores an' looked for you." He shook his head ponderously and put on a long face. "Like looking for a white rabbit in a snowstorm." He doffed his Stetson.

Rebecca rode into the corral, slid from the saddle, and tossed Vermilion's reins to Smokey, the only cowboy the stallion would let groom him. "Will you rub him down, please, Smokey? Father will be a bear if I don't change and get to supper on time."

"How come you're so late?" Smokey cocked a laconic dark eyebrow at her.

All the girl's earlier fury returned. "Skunk Hayes followed me to the promontory."

Smokey jerked straight; his teasing fled. "What'd he want?"

A mischievous devil prompted Rebecca to say, "Me." She regretted it instantly.

Smokey's lips thinned to a slit. His eyelids half closed, and he drawled, "One of these days, me an' Hayes are going to have to have a little talk." His face turned to steel. "Even if he is the boss around here."

A little bell rang deep in Rebecca's mind but not loudly enough for her to figure out why. She grabbed Smokey's checkered sleeve and tugged. "Don't start anything. Please. He'll send you away and —"

"Would you care?" The cowboy stood bareheaded before her, face curiously still.

"You know I would." Her lips trembled. "Sometimes I feel like you're the only friend I have on the Lazy F."

"Good enough for me." Smokey relaxed

and smiled at her.

She pretended not to hear his almost indiscernible "for now" when he led her horse toward the gigantic barn. Rebecca seldom allowed Vermilion the privilege of open grazing. She had seen too many avaricious riders examine her mount's every point and would take no chances on risking Vermilion's loss.

A few paces away, Smokey stopped and glanced back at her. "You know the reason you don't have all the friends you'd like, don't you?" He did not wait for her response. "Your daddy's never cottoned to us cowpokes hanging around."

Red flags waved in her face. "I don't see that it's stopped you," she shot back.

Smokey immediately reverted to his laconic self. "That's 'cause I'm the best shot, the best rider, and the best roper in northern New Mexico."

"Talk about stuck on yourself!" Rebecca made a gamine face at him. "Besides, I can outride you any day."

"Only on Vermilion," he reminded. He scratched his head. "I'll be hanged why I gave away the best horse I'll ever straddle to a braggy girl who thinks she's a real cowpoke."

Rebecca's merry trill brought a sympathetic grin to his rueful face. "Thanks for rubbing Vermilion down," she told him, then ran toward the sprawling log house a hundred yards away.

Formed in the shape of a crude "H," the weathered logs, chinked with thick adobe, had silvered with summer sun until their pale, rounded sides gleamed. Years before, when he took possession, Samuel Fairfax had wisely kept the original house and added to it. Wide porches across the front and west offered a view second only to the one Rebecca saw from the promontory. As usual, she paused and looked back, awed by the magnitude of this part of New Mexico. Could she ever live anywhere else?

Impatiently, she opened the huge front door and stepped inside. No plastered or wallpapered walls greeted her. Just white-washed logs hung with hunting trophies and a smooth floor covered with bearskin rugs both brightened by fantastically designed Indian blankets on couches and chairs.

"Daughter?" Heavy steps from the left arm of the "H" where Samuel had his room preceded her father's entrance into the living area that took up the full front half of the crossbar. Behind it lay an enormous kitchen and Mrs. Cook's quarters.

"Cook by name, cook by trade," the

round-faced woman said when she hired on at the Lazy F shortly after Samuel advertised. "Not for a bunch of roughnecks, though. It's understood that I cook for the family only, plus keep the house clean." She fondly repeated the story during Rebecca's growing-up years. Each time Mrs. Cook grew bolder, though, her boss grew more timid.

The girl loved her too much to admit she had trouble believing her father "just up and lay down and rolled over like a pup," so she merely chuckled and told Mrs. Cook how lucky they were to have her.

"There's plenty of others who'd be glad for my services," Mrs. Cook always said darkly. "Folks who won't be prying into what doesn't concern them."

Rebecca knew it would take an avalanche to uproot their cook/housekeeper, but the threat of her leaving served as an excuse not to ask about a possible Mr. Cook.

"Rebecca?" Samuel stepped into the living room and frowned with displeasure. "Why aren't you ready for supper? I won't have you at the table wearing riding clothes."

With the new awareness that had been growing since she turned eighteen, Rebecca surveyed him through the eyes of a stranger.

Not quite six feet tall, he could be anywhere between forty and fifty; she had learned early not to ask questions. About 180 pounds, with not an ounce of fat, blue eyes, and graying brown hair, he wore the face of an old man on a remarkably strong and healthy body.

"I asked you a question." Not a flicker of love showed, although Rebecca knew she represented the only object in his life that could soften him.

Resentment crisped her reply. "I'd be ready if Clyde Hayes hadn't waylaid me." She ignored the storm signals that sprang to his face. "Why don't you tell him to lay off? I'm not going to marry him, ever, even if you did tell him I would." Color burned in Samuel's face at her well-placed shot, and she incredulously added, "So he wasn't lying." A pulse beat in her throat. "Father, how dared you do such a thing? He's a . . . a snake." She shuddered, as much at the look in her father's eyes as at the grim prospect of ever belonging to a man like Hayes.

"It's not for you to question your father." He retreated into the coldness that normally brought her to heel. "Hayes can run the Lazy F when I'm gone. You can't. You may as well get used to the idea."

Did she dare tell him Hayes had tried to manhandle her on the way home from Raton? She opened her mouth . . . closed it again. If he believed her, he would kill Hayes. No matter how much she hated him, she would not have blood spilled on her account. "I'll go change."

"See that you do," he told her dictatorially.

She turned toward the right arm of the "H" where the western sun sent slanting rays into her room and the storerooms. His voice stopped her in the doorway.

"I don't want you riding out with Travis again. He's in love with you, and I won't have it. Do you hear?"

Rebecca whirled. Her hands clenched into fists, and she planted her feet apart in a fighting posture. "He's the only friend I have on this ranch except Mrs. Cook. Hayes has driven away every cowboy who tried to be nice and friendly. The men barely speak to me. Do you know how it feels to be imprisoned?"

"Has Travis ever laid a hand on you?"

She hated the suspicion in his eyes. "No," she cried. *That's more than I can say for your precious Hayes.* She bit back the inflammatory words. "He respects me too much."

Her father grunted. "Go change your

clothes."

Dismissed, Rebecca felt like a small child being sent to her room. She ran away from her father's presence into the haven of her bedroom and flung herself on the bed. Tears she would not shed before him came in a hot flood. How much longer could she bear his tyranny? Yet — *"Honour thy father and thy mother"* (Exodus 20:12). Where had the words come from? Rebecca believed in God. *Who could live in such a wonderful world and not believe?* But her knowledge of the Bible was vague, although she dimly remembered a woman's voice reading to her. *Had it been my mother? Do the phrases that sometimes spring into my mind have their source in the mists of my past?*

"Rebecca." The muted roar from the living room brought her to her feet. She made a hasty toilet with water, soap, and soft towels that Mrs. Cook must have fetched while Rebecca and her father argued. Then she slipped into a simple white gown, with a modest round neck, that left her arms bare below the elbows. She threw a gaily colored Mexican shawl over her shoulders, opened her door, and started toward the living room. The sound of voices halted her, but she disdainfully went on, dreading but knowing what she would find. Yes, a white-

94

shirted Hayes, with slicked-down mousy hair and reeking to high heaven with pomade, smirked at her from the round table at one end of the living room where meals were served.

She almost fled to her room. Instead, she lifted her chin, gave the unwelcome guest who more and more frequently joined them for the evening meal a cold nod, and slipped into her chair. At least he had not held the chair for her, the lout.

All through the meal she answered in monosyllables, only when spoken to directly. Not by the flicker of an eyelash did she betray that Mrs. Cook's finest roast beef, mouthwatering rolls, and accompanying vegetables tasted like moldy sawdust to her. The moment she choked down the ambrosia pudding, she pushed back her chair.

"May I be excused, please, Father?" She rose, slim and remote in her white gown and gorgeous shawl. "Mrs. Cook promised to show me a new knitting stitch."

"Not very friendly of you to run off when I'm here," Hayes drawled.

His effrontery stung her to quick but guarded speech. She forced a brilliant smile. "But I've already seen you today, Mr. Hayes." She did not dare put him in his place by calling him Hayes as she usually did except when in the presence of her father. "Or have you forgotten so soon?" She laughed maliciously. "Father, would you believe your conscientious foreman took time to ride all the way to the promontory to talk with me instead of making sure the boys got those draws combed?" Before either man could answer the taunt, she vanished into the kitchen, eyes blazing, and carefully closed the door behind her without slamming it. "I just can't bear it," she burst out.

Mrs. Cook looked up from a pan of soapy water. Suds sparkled on her plump hands and glinted from the worn gold band on the third finger of her left hand. Her shrewd, blue eyes held welcome and sympathy. "You always have me, Child."

"I know." Rebecca crossed the kitchen and hugged the housekeeper, heedless of the flying soap bubbles that rose. "If I didn't, I . . . I . . . I'd run away with Smokey Travis!"

"Now why would you want to go and do that?" the buxom woman asked, eyebrows arching almost to her brown hair, dusted with silver that shone in the lamplight. "You're not in love with him, at least not the way you need to be when you marry." She dried her hands on a towel, hugged Rebecca, then held the girl away from her.

"Child, marriage can be wonderful with the right man or miserable with —"

"Hayes." Rebecca's shoulders shook; her face whitened. "Wouldn't it be better to marry Smokey, even if I don't love him the way you say I should, than to be with Hayes? I'd rather be dead."

Mrs. Cook led her to a small table with two chairs. She gently pushed the weeping girl into one of the chairs, then billowed into the other. "And I'd rather see you dead than married to a varmint like him." Her hand, still warm from the dishwater, stroked the girl's hair. "On the other hand, it wouldn't be right or fair to Smokey for you to up and run off with him just to get away from Hayes."

Rebecca looked up and through her tears saw the puzzled expression in Mrs. Cook's face before the good woman slowly said, "I can't understand why your father's so intent about you marrying Clyde Hayes. It's almost as if our foreman knows some secret Samuel Fairfax doesn't want let out."

"Why, that's what I was thinking earlier today." Rebecca straightened and mopped her face with a handkerchief that Mrs. Cook offered her. "Smokey said something funny, too." She wrinkled her forehead, trying to remember exactly what it was. "No use. It's

97

lost. Mrs. Cook, what would you do if you were me?"

For a long time, the housekeeper did not answer. A shadow crept into her blue eyes, darkening them. Finally she said, "First I'd ask God to help me get things straightened out; then I'd keep my eyes peeled every minute and my ears wide open. There's a lot going on around the Lazy F that I can't figure out, but I have my suspicions."

"What are they?" Rebecca leaned forward and whispered.

"It's not for me to say, at least not just yet."

Disappointed, the girl pounced on the first suggestion. "Does God help or even care about me?"

A look of reproach left her feeling scorched with shame when Mrs. Cook quietly told her, "You know better than that. If there's one thing I've taught you in all the years on the Lazy F, it's that God loves everyone and it's up to us to believe it." Her voice changed to a deceptively bland tone. "Of course, it's a lot easier to talk to Him when we know we're His children, and that only comes after we invite His Son to live in our hearts."

Longing rose in Rebecca. "I'm so tired of fighting. I wish I could, but —" A vision of the smirking Hayes danced in the warm kitchen. "He wouldn't want to live in my heart. It's too filled with hate for Hayes," she bitterly said.

"I don't like Hayes, either," Mrs. Cook admitted. "Just remember, we can despise what folks do, but God says we can't hate the miserable sinners who are trying our patience." She stood, looked at a watch she drew from beneath her apron. "Too late for the knitting lesson. Off to bed with you, Child, and don't forget to talk to God."

Rebecca did not answer. It would only hurt Mrs. Cook to know how many times her darling had talked to God and found that He did not answer. She sighed. Perhaps it would not hurt to try again. Things could not get much worse, or she would do something awful.

"God, I'm in the middle of a mess," she stated frankly when she had climbed into a nightgown and knelt by her bed. "I don't even know how to pray." Dissatisfied but void of words, she quickly said, "Amen," and got into bed.

Her outdoor life provided exercise enough to put her to sleep immediately, but first she remembered Smokey's words. *Even if he is the boss around here.* She sat bolt upright. *Why did Smokey think Hayes was boss, not Father?*

CHAPTER 6

Among the hundreds of beautiful places to ride on the Lazy F, one lured Rebecca again and again. The day after her encounter with Hayes, she expertly saddled and mounted Vermilion. Warm spring sun had blossomed the range into meadows of flowers. Cottonwood and willows along the stream born in the mountains that ran through Fairfax's land and never went dry whispered secrets. In the east, the Old Trail continued its never-ending way with its sister, the Cimarron, and the sloping range smoothed into an endless prairie gray. Melting snow patches on the mountains above smiled down on the girl and her horse as they weaved their way up steep sides until they rode through groves of aspens that quivered with every breeze.

Rebecca and Vermilion emerged from the grove onto a promontory. "Whoa." She pulled lightly on the reins and wheeled the red stallion. Never did she take this particular ride without turning to look over the valley floor. The ranch in the distance looked small by comparison with the vast world spread below her.

A Mexican village she seldom was allowed to visit huddled its adobe houses together as if for protection against danger. She remembered a fiesta day, the colorful clothing, strum of guitars, and happy dancing from a year before and laughed at the way she had deliberately slipped away from home in defiance of Samuel Fairfax's orders.

"It was worth being shut up in my room for three days," she confessed to Vermilion, with a toss of her head that dislodged her sombrero and tumbled her nut-brown hair around her laughing face. The merry sparkle left her eyes. "Why doesn't Father want me to visit the village? Or ride to the neighbors?"

Vermilion shook his head, and his reddish mane brushed the girl's gloved hand.

She patted him. "I know you want to go. You're thinking about the lush green grass at Lone Man Cabin." In spite of the warm day, a shiver went through her, but she nudged Vermilion into a trot and climbed the slope to a small pass that lay above her destination. Lone Man Cabin stood in a grove of white-trunked aspens in the heart of a canyon. It had been built years before by a settler who had been killed by hostile Indians before peace came to New Mexico. A shining stream intersected the aspen grove and ran beside the dilapidated shack that, nevertheless, held a morbid fascination for Rebecca. The gobble of a wild turkey, from a thicket to her left, brought a thrill to her nature-loving heart, and she called, "Run, you white-tailed beauty!" to a graceful antelope that sprang from its grazing and bounded away at the crack of Vermilion's hooves on rock.

Minutes later, they paused by Lone Man Creek. Rebecca slid from the saddle, threw herself flat, and drank her fill of the icy water while Vermilion splashed into the stream below her, then lowered his head to drink. Satisfied, he sent up sprays of water, lunged out of the creek, and grazed, no stranger to this haunted, lovely spot.

Something about the place felt strange, not like its usual air of solitude that both fascinated and repelled the girl. She rose to investigate, walked past the cabin, and stopped short.

A fence of peeled poles, still oozing, stretched from slope to slope. A wide, closed gate kept horses and cattle from straying.

"Why, there's never been a fence here before!" Rebecca took an involuntary step toward the gate.

"Stop right there, little missy." Words harsh as the black-browed man who glided out of a clump of aspens froze her to the ground.

"Who are you, and what are you doing on the Lazy F?" she demanded, more angry than frightened. "What's this fence doing here, and why are those horses and cattle penned?"

"Beggin' your pardon, Missy, but that's my business, not yours."

"It *is* my business." Using the quick draw Smokey Travis had taught her, Rebecca pulled the small but deadly weapon she always carried and pointed it rock-steady at the intruder. "I'm Rebecca Fairfax, and this is my father's land."

A curious whistling sound alerted her, but too late. A noose sang and dropped over her head and shoulders, pinning her arms to her side with a tightening jerk that loosened her fingers until the pistol dropped. The next instant, she lay on the ground, securely bound.

The black-browed man leered down at her. "So, Missy, thought you'd hold me up, did you?" He bent, and she flinched from the smell of sweat and his whiskey breath. "Now, there ain't no use of you bellerin', so I won't gag you. Just keep your mouth shut, and you won't get hurt." He blindfolded her and laughed crudely. "My pard's pertic'ler about folks seein' his face."

Deprived of sight, Rebecca's other senses intensified. She strained her ears, trying to hear above the hard pound of her heart. *Who is the second man, the one who roped me and doesn't want to be seen?*

Hayes! The word shot into her brain like sunlight into a dark well. It drove out the fear that had paralyzed her when the evil-looking man stood over her. Bad as she suspected Hayes to be, he would not stand for any man except himself to maul her. So she lay still, motionless except for her cautious exploring fingers behind her back that tried to pick at the knots and loosen the lariat.

If I can get even one hand free, I'll snatch the blindfold off and get a good look at Hayes, she promised herself. Her plan did not work. Hayes, or whoever had tied those knots, obviously did not take chances. She could not budge them. Her mind steadied, considered, and rejected a half-dozen plans. Suddenly, hot blood pumped from her heart in a spurt of determination. She had it! Turning her head to one side, Rebecca slowly rubbed her face against the ground, flinching when dirt imbedded in her cheek but gradually working the blindfold up far enough for her to see.

She had been right. Hayes and the man who had accosted her by the fence stood several yards away in low conversation. Once, Hayes glanced at her, and she stilled and closed her eyes, praying he would not notice the position of the blindfold. He looked angry, yet something in his manner told Rebecca he was pleading with the other man. Again, she listened intensely and managed to catch a few words. ". . . didn't see me . . . you lay low . . . we'll meet. . . ."

Hayes turned abruptly and walked out of her line of vision. Rebecca did not dare move her head, but her keen ears picked up the creak of saddle leather, then guarded hoofbeats that increased into a diminishing drum. She thought of the look the black-browed man had given her and almost called out. Better to take her chances with Hayes than be left here with his partner.

"Sorry, Missy." Cold steel slipped between her wrists and cut the lariat; a rude hand snatched the blindfold from her eyes. "I didn't reckon you were really Sam Fairfax's girl." He laughed uneasily, and something flickered in his eyes. Rebecca knew he had lied. "A feller can't be too careful," he went on.

She stood and brushed debris from her riding habit. "My father will hear of this outrage," she furiously told him. She bit her tongue to keep from flinging out that she knew Clyde Hayes was involved in whatever nefarious scheme this turned out to be.

"I wouldn't say anythin' if I was you." The black-browed man opened his sheep-lined coat and showed a badge of some kind. "I've been appointed to look into the rustlin' that's goin' on, and a purty little thing like you wouldn't want to throw a hitch into my 'nvestigations, now would you?"

Not for a minute did she believe him. Yet, when Rebecca thought of the isolation, she wisely did not argue. Mrs. Cook always said there were more ways than one to skin a cat. Rebecca did an about-face and became the helpless female who is impressed with the law. "Oh, my, I can see why you couldn't have me interfering!" She gave him a dazzling smile that successfully masked her fear and disgust. "Deputy — it is *deputy*, isn't it?"

"Dep'ty Crowley." He half closed his eyes,

and she saw suspicion in their murky depths.

"It's just that I got such a shock, seeing the fence and all." She nodded toward the newly erected barrier. Her frankness lightened the deputy's face, and she went on, "If I'd known you were an honest-to-goodness law officer, I wouldn't have pulled my gun." She almost choked, wondering if he would swallow that, even though what she said was true. "Is the other man a deputy, too?"

"Naw." Crowley spat a stream of tobacco juice dangerously close to his boot. "He's what you might call an intr'sted party." He pulled a plug of tobacco from his shirt pocket, cut off a quid, and stored it in his cheek.

Rebecca wanted to laugh. It made him look like a lopsided chipmunk. Instead, she delicately shuddered. "This has all been most upsetting." She managed a feeble smile that should convince the bogus deputy of her helplessness. "I suppose the corral and the horses and cattle are all part of your plan to catch rustlers?" She hoped her naïve question would disarm him.

"Uh, yeah. That's why it's 'mportant for you to keep mum." His gaze bored into her, and she suddenly felt more afraid than ever.

"I won't tell Father right away," she promised. "You'll probably get your job done soon, and then it won't matter who knows."

A hasty hand to Crowley's mouth half concealed his grin. "You're right, Missy. My job'll be done soon, and it won't matter."

Her cheek smarted from ground-in dirt, and her fingers itched to slap his leering face, but Rebecca chose the better part. "Good-bye, Mr., uh, Deputy Crowley." She turned and walked to Vermilion, who had finished grazing and now stood waiting for her. She put her left foot in the stirrup and swung her right leg across the saddle.

Crowley's voice stopped her. "Say, how about tradin' horses?" His eyes gleamed with the lust for good horseflesh that she had seen dozens of times before when rough men saw Vermilion. "This stallion's too big for such a little girl as you. Now, my mare there —" He nodded at a piebald horse Rebecca would not have ridden to an outhouse. "She's just your size."

What a credulous fool he considered her. Well, that image might just be her best protection. When he stepped in front of Vermilion, Rebecca overcame her desire to ride the man down and cried out, "Oh, be careful! Vermilion only allows me and the

109

cowboy who broke him to handle him." The horse raised both feet in the air to prove her point, and Crowley leaped aside.

"I'd take that out of him," he muttered.

Rebecca brought her horse down and started back through the aspens. "I couldn't sell Vermilion, even to you, Deputy Crowley, but I see you know a good horse when you see one." She wanted to pointedly gaze at the corralled animals but restrained herself. Right now, getting away meant continuing the role she had chosen.

"If you ever change your mind, I'll be waitin'," he called after her.

Thoroughly disgusted, Rebecca did not answer. She used the long miles back to the ranch house to mull over everything that had happened. A half mile from home, the clatter of hooves warned that someone desperately planned to overtake her. A quick glance behind showed Hayes riding bent over the muscular neck of the racing bay he unimaginatively had christened Bay. She fought the impulse to outrun him and composed herself. A little voice inside whispered the significance of this meeting. Under no circumstances must Hayes discover that she had recognized him back at Lone Man Cabin.

"Ho, Becky." He swung up beside her and

tipped his Stetson. "Have a nice ride?"

"Splendid. I went clear to Lone Man Cabin. Too bad someone doesn't build a house there. It's the prettiest place around."

"I'll start layin' the foundation tomorrow if you say the word." He pulled Bay closer and laid one hand over hers on the saddle horn where her hand rested. "Say, what happened to your face?"

Rebecca unobtrusively nudged Vermilion with her boot heel, and he danced away, leaving Hayes trying to control Bay, who feared the big red stallion along with most of the other Lazy F horses. "I hit the ground. And I told you I won't marry you."

"Girls change," he doggedly said. "How about forgiv'n' me for last fall?"

Could he really be so thick-headed he thought the only reason she hated him was because of his actions on the way home from Raton when he had been drinking? "Hayes, why don't you find a woman close to your age instead of hanging after me?" she blurted out.

His face darkened, and she knew her taunt had been a mistake. Before he could reply, she innocently asked, "Why, where's your lariat?" She pointed to Bay's saddle horn.

It distracted him, as she had known it would do. Hayes stammered and finally said, "Left it in the bunkhouse, I guess. Yeah, that's right. One of the hands sneaked it out and brought it back soaked. When I find out who, there'll be one less hand on the Lazy F."

She could not resist saying, "I thought we needed every hand we could get. I heard Father telling you to hire all the vaqueros from the Mexican village for spring roundup."

"Maybe I'll wait until after roundup." He lapsed into sullen silence, then asked, "How was everythin' at Lone Man Cabin?"

Rebecca feigned surprise. "Why? Should there be anything wrong?" She saw the quickly hidden but satisfied look in Hayes's eyes and knew it had been his idea for "Deputy Crowley" to swear her to silence about the peeled pole fence, raw in its newness.

"I just haven't ridden out there lately. Guess I should one of these days. Sometimes cattle and horses drift down the canyon by Lone Man Creek." His false laugh could not have fooled Vermilion. "Strange how dumb the critters are. They drift in but not out!"

Not so strange when they are corralled, Rebecca wanted to shout. Instead, she said, "Maybe you and some of the boys should check the canyon. I did see horses and cattle."

They reached the ranch house in time for her to escape more conversation with Hayes. As usual, Smokey Travis waited on the top rail of the corral.

"Travis, why are you sittin' there like a prairie hen on a nest?" Hayes blared, while his nondescript eyes flashed.

Dull red suffused the cowboy's brown face, and he started to speak. Behind Hayes's back, Rebecca shook her head slightly in warning. Smokey's face broke into a smile. "I'm waitin' for you, Boss, an' am glad to tell you we found most a hundred head of cattle up a draw. They must have wandered in there last fall. Anyway, we put the Lazy F brand on at least a dozen new calves and herded the whole kit and caboodle back down with the main herd." His gaze turned to Rebecca's face, and his eyes flashed.

The tension drained from Hayes's shoulders. Overbearing, even crooked he might be, but he loved the range and cattle. "That's good news." He slid off Bay, yanked off the saddle, and gave the horse a slap that sent him whinnying into the pasture nearby. "Fairfax aims to make a killin' on

113

the roundup this spring. The more we sell, the fewer that'll fall to rustlin'."

Smokey had a coughing spell that left him red-faced and teary-eyed. "Sorry, Boss, Miss Rebecca. Must have picked up some dust in my throat." He leaped down from the fence. "I'll take care of Vermilion, if you like," he told the girl.

She started to protest and thought better of it. While she could and did perfectly groom her own horse, she knew Smokey loved Vermilion as much as she did. "Thanks, Sm— Travis," she quickly corrected. She had learned long ago that calling the cowboys by their first names made her father and Hayes furious. No use rousing their ire, especially when she had a secret. The less attention they paid her, the freer she would be to solve the mystery of Lone Man Cabin and the newly constructed fence. She burned to tell Smokey what had happened. She had promised not to report to her father about being waylaid and the developments in Lone Man Canyon but had carefully omitted any promise about not telling Smokey.

How could she get a message to him? When Father was not watching her, Hayes replaced the vigilance. Even when she did not see them, she felt their spying. Well, she could be clever, too.

After supper and dishes, while the two voices rumbled in the big living room, Rebecca covered her white gown with a long, dark cloak that hid every trace of it and allowed her to become just another dark shadow in the night. Praying for luck to find Smokey alone, she groped her way to the bunkhouse and peered in a window. She counted off the hands, from Curly the cook, to Jim, who had been with the Lazy F just a few weeks but long enough to learn that friendliness beyond a nod and "howdy" with the daughter of the house was not permitted. All accounted for — except Smokey.

An iron hand covered her lips. Another jerked her away from the window and into a clump of cottonwoods. "Who're you, an' why're you spying?" someone hissed. Rebecca found herself spun around. *God, help me,* she silently prayed. *If Father or Hayes is holding me, what will happen?*

Strong hands pulled her closer. Miserly light from the edge of the moon that rose over the mountain spilled onto the dark-clad figure, the man who held her. "Rebecca, what are you *doing* out here?"

She sagged in relief and would have fallen if not for his support. "Smokey, thank God!"

"Shh." He picked her up bodily and

stepped deep into the dark shelter of the cottonwood grove. Again, he placed his hand over her lips, but gently this time. Screened by leaves filtering pale moonlight that brightened as Hayes and Fairfax stood smoking on the ranch house porch, she scarcely breathed. She could feel Smokey's deadly calm body coiled ready to spring in her defense. A lifetime later, Fairfax went inside and slammed the door; Hayes marched very close past them. Not until a light came on in the bunkhouse room, which was set apart from the long, tiered-bunk sleeping quarters of the rest of the men, did Smokey remove his hand.

"Sorry. But how'd I know you'd do such a fool thing?"

"I was looking for you," she whispered. In quick sentences, Rebecca told him what had happened from the moment she saw the fence in Lone Man Canyon until she and Hayes reached the corral.

"Why, that skunk!" Smokey shook with rage. "He roped you? I'm gonna call him out right now, and —" He tore free from her involuntary grasp and took a quick step out of their hiding place.

"Smokey, no!" Quicker than a mountain lion, she slid in front of him. "I won't have you kill because of me." She grabbed his arms with hands made strong by fear. "There's a better way to get Hayes. Don't you see? We'll watch and spy and expose his rustling, for I'm sure that's what he's doing."

"Your daddy will never believe it." He stood stock-still in her grip. Enough light sneaked past the trees to show his whitened face and inscrutable dark eyes that could dance with mischief but now looked hard and cold, relentless.

Rebecca shivered. "He will have to. I don't believe Crowley's a deputy any more than you are."

She felt Smokey give a convulsive start before he said in an odd voice, "That's — you'd better go in, Rebecca." His voice changed. "I . . . I'm glad you told me."

"So am I, Smokey. Sometimes I feel the only one who really knows or understands me is God."

He parted branches, checked both ways, then ran with her across the lighted yard to a side door in the right arm of the house where she could slip into a storeroom, then get to her bedroom, unobserved. At the doorway, he leaned down, awkwardly planted a kiss on her forehead, and said, "That's just to let you know God an' me are both on your side." Then he swung away with a remarkably light tread for a man who spent most of his waking hours in the saddle, leaving Rebecca staring after him and feeling less alone now that she had shared her heavy secret.

CHAPTER 7

Sometimes, Joel felt he had been riding forever. Querida scrambled up a game trail and came out on a mesa. Her owner gasped. What a view! Grand country, this New Mexican land. He had been told in Santa Fe what to expect, yet from the backbone of the tableland, between the mountains and foothills, the range curved in a half moon, walled by the Rockies. Dark, timber-sloped gullies joined cedar ridges; a bleached moon cast its pale light. No sign of human habitation for as far as Joel could see; just empty miles unrolling around him.

"We camp out again tonight, Querida." His old habit of talking to his horse and a cheerful whistle brought an answering nicker from Querida, who, freed from saddle and blanket, rolled in spring grass and then contentedly settled to graze.

A crackling fire, a meager meal of toasted biscuits and the last of his dried beef topped off by a treasured tin of peaches, brought a sigh of satisfaction. "Nothing like a meal to lift spirits. Right, old girl?"

Querida raised her head, then went back to munching.

Joel laughed, yet a certain wistfulness shone in his eyes. He washed his few eating utensils, spread blankets on the ground near his fire, and stared into the dying blaze. Now that night surrounded him, even the food could not fend off discouragement. Six months earlier, he had preached in San Scipio with startling results. Now, he rested his head on his saddle and stared at the starry sky, remembering that fateful Sabbath.

For some reason, Joel had struggled with finding a text more than at any other time he prepared a sermon. He considered and discarded a full dozen, settling on one, then another. Yet, all through his study, the words of Jesus in Matthew 5:23–24 remained present. How could he step into a strange pulpit and preach on that text? Yet, how could he deny what he felt led to say?

Refusing breakfast on the gorgeous West Texas autumn morning, he rode to town on Querida, still struggling. Early as he was, a crowd had preceded him. He remembered many of the faces and recognized others' names. One tall, thin, tired-looking woman with straw-colored hair and washed-out gray eyes approached him. She wore clothing more suitable to a young girl than to a woman nearing forty.

"You look just like your dear uncle," she gushed. "Gideon and I were sweethearts years ago." She giggled girlishly.

The grotesque sound, coming from this faded blossom trying to cling to the past, brought a startled, "Really!" from Joel.

"Oh, yes," she chortled, making no effort to lower her voice.

"I'm Lucinda — used to be Curtis. I'm sure dear Gideon has spoken of me."

Joel thanked heaven for the control he had learned over the years that now kept him from laughing at the pathetic woman. Gideon had indeed spoken of Lucinda, sharing how even though he felt sorry for her, she had made his stay in San Scipio as a preacher unbearable with her chasing.

"It's nice you could come, Miss . . . Mrs. . . . ," he managed to say while she pumped his hand up and down.

"Mrs. Baker." She looked skyward and dragged a meek little man forward. "My husband, these past ten years." She gave the man no chance to speak. "Do remember me to your uncle when you see him again."

With an arch smile, she took her husband by the arm. "Come along, or we won't get the front pew." He trotted obediently after her, the way a fawn followed a doe.

"Sweethearts, my eye," someone whispered behind Joel. "Leave it to Lucinda Curtis Baker to kick up a cyclone when there's no more wind than from slamming a door!"

Joel repressed a smile and greeted the next person. After folks stopped coming and every seat was filled and men were standing at the back, the San Scipio minister introduced Joel. "You all remember Gideon Scott, Elijah and Naomi's son. This is his nephew, the Scotts' grandson. I've asked him to bring the Word of the Lord to us today. Brother Joel, you have our careful and prayerful attention."

Joel found it hard to begin. His heart went out to Lige, who sat rigid at the introduction that made no mention of the long-missing real father. Yet Joel had a feeling the text that had been impressed on him was not for Lige's benefit. He opened the worn Bible that traveled on Querida wherever Joel rode. " 'Therefore if thou bring thy gift to the altar, and there rememberest that thy brother hath ought against thee; leave there thy gift before the altar, and go thy way;

first be reconciled to thy brother, and then come and offer thy gift.' " He closed the Bible and leaned forward against the sturdy, handmade pulpit. "I don't know why Matthew 5:23 and 24 has driven all other Scripture passages from my mind and heart ever since I knew I would preach to you." He saw looks of surprise and exchanged glances.

"Perhaps it is because every one of us at times realizes someone, somewhere, has something against us. We may have offended our brothers and sisters years ago and not even recognized it. Or, we may secretly know of times when we spoke unkind words that cut a tender heart." Joel continued preaching in a clear, simple manner, using the thoughts he felt coming. He referred to the healing that comes to both when a child of God seeks out one wronged.

He concluded, "If anything in your life is keeping your gift at the altar from being acceptable to God, make it right." He paused to be sure nothing more needed saying, then sat down.

"Let us pray," the San Scipio minister said. He offered one of the humblest, most beautiful prayers Joel had ever heard and followed it by leading the young guest minister to the back of the church to greet the congregation as they left.

A good half hour later, everyone except Lucinda had gone after having shaken Joel's hand and wishing him Godspeed. Even the meek Mr. Baker silently shook hands, then slipped out.

"Why, Lucinda, you're still here?" The minister turned.

Red-eyed and swollen-faced, the woman said, "I must talk with the Reverend Scott."

Joel cringed. He hated being called Reverend and set apart as some holier-than-others being. He also did not care for a private interview with the woman. Yet, none of her former kittenish attitude remained. His heart went out to her, as it did to anyone in trouble. "Tell my grandparents I'll be home soon," he said to the minister. The other man nodded and left, closing the door behind him.

"What is it, Mrs. Baker?"

Fresh tears poured. "I . . . I've done something terrible." She pressed her hands to her twisting face. "All these years, I should have spoken." The hands fell and revealed a tragic face filled with regret. "I knew, but I didn't want to . . . and then he was gone, and I hated Judith for marrying Gideon. . . ."

He could not make sense of her broken

confession. "What is it you know?" he gently asked.

"Cyrus Scott. He . . . he . . ." The cloudburst came again.

Joel had always thought novels that said someone's heart stood still were the height of stupidity. Now, he experienced that very thing. He could not speak. He could not breathe. Not until hope for a long-hidden clue to his father's disappearance loosed him to action could he do more than stare at the repentant woman. "What do you know of him?" he inquired hoarsely.

She blew her nose and raised her head. Remorse lent depth to the gray eyes. "The night before he . . . he left, I saw him." Dying sobs still racked her thin frame. "I . . . I thought he was Gideon, and I called out. He was riding toward the ranch. He wheeled his horse, and when I saw who it was, I asked him to tell Gideon how thrilled the town was with his preaching." She sniffed.

"What did he say?" Joel's head spun. Had this vindictive woman held the key to Cyrus's whereabouts all these long years?

"He . . . he laughed in that hateful way he had and said he wasn't a messenger boy for his brother. When he turned back toward the ranch, he laughed again, mocking me, and said, 'Besides, I'm off to Albuquerque.

125

Too bad I can't take Gideon with me and get him away from simpering females like you.' " Anguish filled her voice. "I made up my mind I'd die before helping him or ever telling anyone what he said." She crossed her arms over her thin chest and threw back her head. "I kept that promise until today. But when you read those verses, I knew God meant them for me." Her voice trailed to a whisper.

Hot anger over her silence melted into pity. Her eyes showed long-held pain and what it had cost her to speak. Joel put a warm, strong hand on one of her cold ones. "Mrs. Baker — Lucinda — all we can do to atone of the things we do or leave undone is to repent. That's the wonder of God's grace, that He forgives. Now, you must forgive yourself."

"Should I stand up in meeting next week and confess?"

He knew she would do it but shook his head. "No. I will tell my grandparents, but it would only cause more pain to have San Scipio hashing it over again. Tell your husband, and then accept God's forgiveness."

Something akin to glory gradually crept into her face, and when Lucinda Curtis Baker walked out of the church to her

126

patient, waiting husband, Joel swallowed hard. Thank God for His power that had changed the foolish woman who entered church that day into the new creature who went out.

He shook his head at his musing and, with a glad heart, raced Querida back to the Circle S. His shocking announcement precipitated a crisis. Life flowed back into Lige Scott's face, and he nearly reneged on his promise to take Naomi west.

"Don't you see," he protested, "now we have something to go on, a starting place. Naomi, how can I go to Arizona when Cyrus may be alive and needing me?"

"Your younger son needs you, too, Lige," she quietly reminded. "Will you again choose Cyrus over Gideon?"

He flinched as if she had struck him, and Joel stepped in.

"Grandpa." His face shone with boyish eagerness. He gripped Lige's brawny arm. "If Cyrus is alive, I mean to find him; I vowed that when I left Flagstaff. Gideon needs you. All these years he's longed to see you and blot out the anger between you when he left. We don't know that my . . . my father is in New Mexico. He may have changed his mind or drifted there and gone elsewhere. Can't you trust me to seek him out?" He licked dry lips. "I believe God will help me."

The moment stretched into infinity before Lige bowed his head to a force greater than his own. "Son, I trust you. Naomi and I will catch the train from El Paso as soon as we can get there."

"Do you want me to take you?" Joel offered.

Lige shook his massive head. "No. The sooner you go, the better." He lifted both arms and let his huge hands drop on Joel's shoulders. "Go with God, Joel."

The howl of a distant coyote calling for its mate roused Joel from his reverie. He threw more wood on the fire and pulled his blankets closer against the cold spring night. The long day of riding should have left him weary. Instead, he remained sleepless, even when he closed his eyes against the display of stars hanging low in the sky. How high his hopes had been when he departed from the Circle S a few hours after Lige and Naomi boarded the stage for El Paso!

With youthful exuberance, he ignored the interminable years that stretched between Cyrus's flight from the discovery of his cruel deception and Joel's return to the ranch. He debated leaving Querida on the Circle S and going by train to New Mexico but discarded the idea immediately. He had no guarantee his father had ever reached Albuquerque or that it had not been merely a picturesque stopping place.

While Joel disconsolately reviewed the history of New Mexico, frost gathered and sparkled the range with diamond dust. Cyrus had ridden away in 1874, the same year that opened the bloodiest years of western history in eastern and central New Mexico. Between then and 1879, more desperate and vicious men than could be counted terrorized the land. Three hundred men died in the Lincoln County War that pitted rustlers, desperadoes, and cattlemen, honest and crooked, against each other. Billy the Kid boasted twenty-one killings. Sentenced to be hanged in April 1881, he killed two deputies, escaped, then was killed by Pat Garrett in July — at the age of twenty.

Geronimo, one of the last of the hostile Apache chiefs, added to the terror until his surrender in 1886. During the late 1870s, the territorial governor, General Lew Wallace, called on martial law and used troops to end the bloodbath.

Gloom dropped like a tarpaulin over Joel. Could Cyrus, with his wild love of adventure, have escaped the violence and death of those turbulent New Mexico territorial days? Or did his bones lie in some unmarked grave on the "lone prairie" along with countless others who lived and died by the sword?

In the dark hour between the waning moon and the gray dusk that heralds the dawn, when bodies and minds are at their lowest ebb, Joel Scott faced the truth. He might not be able to keep his vow. He had planned every bright bit of color concerning his father, only to have it turn to fool's gold, dross, in his hands. Most of the old-timers he talked with had never heard the name Cyrus Scott. One or two had scratched grizzled heads and admitted seeing young fellers now and then with "goldy hair and blue eyes like you'n," but they couldn't recollect any such name as Cyrus.

Joel ranged far and wide, stopping over at ranches and leaving word that if anyone knew of the man he sought, to contact Gideon Scott in Flagstaff; a reward would be forthcoming. Periodically, Joel lighted long enough to send and receive letters. So far, there had been no takers on the reward offer — just two or three false leads that roused great hope and petered out like all the others.

Joel wintered on a ranch not far from

Santa Fe. He won the admiration of the hands with his range skills, the gratitude of plain folk and Mexican families with his preaching on Sundays. When spring came, they reluctantly bid him farewell.

Joel had left the Double J in Arizona in late summer of 1888. In some ways, spring 1890 found him no closer to a solution of the mystery.

Still wide awake, Joel's lips twisted in a wry grin. A few weeks from now, on April 30, he would be twenty years old. He felt at least thirty and far removed from the excited boy who set off to reclaim his father and win him for the Lord. A fierce attack of homesickness assailed him. What he would give to see the Double J, spar with Lonesome and the boys, marvel over how much Matt and Millie, the twins, had grown. When dawn broke, why should he not just saddle Querida and head west? He had acted on the advice of a cowboy from the ranch where he wintered to "ride east into as purty a country as you'll ever see" and ended up agreeing. The hand had added, "I useter work on a swell spread called the Lazy F. Wish I'd never left." Longing softened the planes of his face.

"Why did you?" Joel's keen gaze bored into the other's open, honest countenance.

"Huh, got driv' off by the owner." Amber fire flashed in the cowboy's eyes. "All I did was try an' spark the daughter." His face reddened, but he continued to look directly at Joel. "I only smiled an' talked with her a coupla times. Never even touched her. But Fairfax's foreman, Hayes, told the boss I was sweet on Rebecca. I was," he admitted. Hardness thinned his lips. "At least I didn't mean bad by her."

"Who did?"

The cowboy buttoned his lip, shook his head, then unslitted his mouth just wide enough to say, "I ain't sayin', but I sure feel sorry for any girl Hayes gets his hands on." His oblique, meaningful glance finished the story.

Joel felt pity for the unknown Rebecca and something else. "What's this Hayes like?" he demanded sharply.

"Mean. Mid-thirties. Loco over the girl. Mousy brown hair, gray eyes that make you feel like he's hidin' somethin' all the time. Big jasper, tall as you." He measured Joel with a glance. "You weigh in about 160?"

Joel nodded.

"Hayes has a good forty pounds on you." He cocked his head to one side. "If you ever just happen to mosey up that way, tell Smokey Travis howdy from Jeff."

"I will." Joel's hand shot out. But when he finished packing his saddlebags and mounted Querida, Jeff stepped closer.

"In case you should end up at the Lazy F, keep your eye peeled an' don't never let your horse run loose."

Joel's spine snapped to attention. "Hayes?"

"I never said nothin' a-tall." Jeff half closed his eyes and grinned.

"Thanks for nothin' a-tall," Joel mimicked and turned Querida in the direction the inscrutable cowboy pointed.

Mile by mile, he headed through incredible and varied country until he knew he must be near the Lazy F. The sun yawned, opened its eye a crack, and peered over a mountain. Joel still had not slept. He had to make a decision . . . go or stay. Head home in defeat and take up his lifework of preaching or aimlessly search when every clue had died. Lige and Naomi had fallen in love with the Double J, and the last thing Joel had heard was that they had ordered their foreman to sell the Circle S. Why not join them and forget the father who had never known he had a son?

Still undecided, Joel broke camp. Before he did much more riding anywhere, he needed supplies. He remembered Jeff saying a Mexican village lay on the Lazy F. He could replenish his food, get oats for Querida for a change, and look over the ranch. Time enough then to head out.

Late afternoon found him riding through range inhabited by cattle as far as he could see. Hundreds, no thousands, must be on this rolling, endless, grazing land. He finally reached the line of cottonwoods he knew bordered the stream that ran through the ranch and lay below the ranch house.

Coarse jeers and curses rent the still air, and Joel circled to avoid meeting a group of riders face to face. Something in their hard faces warned him they would not welcome a stranger. Yet, his overdeveloped sense of curiosity forced him to investigate. Admonishing Querida to silence, he slipped from the saddle and led his horse around a willow thicket.

Dear God, no! Thirty feet away, a cowboy who could not be more than a year or so older than Joel straddled a buckskin horse that nervously shifted. The man's hands were tied behind his back. With a thrill of terror, Joel saw the noose around the white-faced cowboy's neck, the big man with a taunting smile who stood with hand upraised to hit the buckskin's flank. *Hayes!* He fit Jeff's description to the last detail.

"Got anythin' to say?" a mounted rider called.

"A lot!" the doomed cowboy yelled. "Hayes knows I'm no rustler. Ask him the real reason he framed me."

"Shut up!" Hayes snatched a Colt from his holster and pointed it.

"Let him talk, Hayes." A murmur of assent ran through the assembled men, and Joel took heart. Evidently, they were not as eager for a hanging as the Lazy F foreman was.

The courageous cowboy whose life hung by a thread shouted, "Ask him about Lone Man Canyon an' a bogus deputy that calls himself Crowley an' how they roped and tied Miss Rebecca —"

In the heartbeat before Hayes moved, guilt blackened his face. The riders froze. "You lyin', thievin' —" Hayes swung his arm high, opened his palm. It exploded with a horrid crack on the buckskin's flank.

The buckskin leaped. A shot rang out and severed the tightened rope. The cowboy, still bound, fell to the ground and lay stunned.

Joel, a gun in each hand, one still smoking, stepped from the thicket and confronted the paralyzed men.

CHAPTER 8

"Howdy, boys." Joel kept his revolvers trained square on the slack-jawed Hayes, whose face had gone a dirty yellow. "Drop the gun, Mister."

Hayes slowly let his unfired Colt drop from his fingers.

Joel shot a lightning glance toward the huddled group of staring riders, stopped at the one who had demanded that the condemned man be allowed to talk, and ordered, "You, there. Untie the boy."

"What is this, a holdup?" Hayes recovered his voice and some of his shaken arrogance. He took one step toward the newcomer.

"Don't you move." Joel's eyes flashed blue fire. He waited until the man on the ground dazedly sat up and rubbed circulation back into his wrists where the rope had cut into them. "What's your name, and what's this all about? Where I come from, we don't hang folks without a mighty good reason."

The contempt in his voice sent angry red into Hayes's face and shame to the still-mounted riders' countenances.

The reprieved cowboy sprang to his feet. Tossed dark hair and scornful dark eyes highlighted his deeply tanned face. "Thanks, Stranger. I'm Smokey Travis. Clyde Hayes is foreman of the Lazy F — you musta seen the brand on a lot of cattle no matter which way you came. He's hated me an' tried to drive me away like he did every hand who's protected Miss Rebecca from him —"

"Jeff, for instance? I rode with him down Santa Fe way, and he said to tell you howdy." Joel's revolvers never wavered, but he caught the pop-eyed look on a half-dozen faces. "Now, you boys lay down your guns real nice and easylike."

A slight movement from Hayes sent steel into Joel's eyes. "I wouldn't try anything if I were you."

"Do as he says," Hayes's hoarse voice bellowed.

Joel waited until the men disarmed, then said over the pounding of his heart, "All right, let's have it." He sheathed his guns.

Smokey stepped up beside him and glared at Hayes. "He's crookeder than a mountain goat trail. Rebecca Fairfax found it out weeks ago an' told me. He's running some

137

kind of double cross on the boss, who thinks so all-fired much of him he won't believe anything but good."

Joel's lips curled. "And the rest of these men?"

"Aw, we sure didn't know anything about a crooked deal — until just now," the cowhand who untied Smokey protested. His clear eyes attested to his honesty, but the dark faces of some of the others indicated that they had known and were neck-deep in the plot against Samuel Fairfax.

"What do you have to say?" Joel wheeled back toward Hayes.

"Lies. Travis has been a burr under the saddle ever since he rode in. I'm goin' to marry Becky, and he's jealous." Hayes spat on the ground.

"That's not what she says," said Smokey.

Joel's lips involuntarily curved upward in sympathy with Travis's mocking smile.

"It's what her daddy says that counts. Now get off the ranch. You're fired. If I ever catch you sneakin' around again, I'll run you in." Hayes stooped to pick up his Colt.

"Hold it." Like magic, Joel's revolvers sprang from his holsters in a draw so fast the crowd of men gasped. "Smokey, pitch those guns into the willow thicket. The men can get them back after we're gone."

"Just who are you, anyway, to come ridin' in where it's none of your business?" Hayes frothed at the mouth.

A slow smile of pure enjoyment crept across Joel's face. He could feel it stretch the skin across his cheekbones. "Why, saving folks is my business. I'm a preacher."

"Huh?" Hayes's exclamation mingled with Smokey's loud, "Whoopee!"

"You mean a preacher got the drop on us?" the clear-eyed cowboy demanded. "Haw, haw!" He rolled on the ground in a paroxysm of mirth.

Hayes screamed, "You're fired, too, Perkins! I knew you wouldn't last when I hired you." His colorless eyes flamed.

Perkins leaped to his feet. "Too late, Boss. I quit when Smokey said you lassoed Miss Rebecca." He looked each of the other riders in the eye. "If any of ya are men, you'll come with me." He waited a moment, but no one moved. "I'd rather ride with a herd of polecats than you. C'mon, Smokey, let's hit the trail. Half-a-dozen ranches around here'll be glad to get us. Preacher, how about comin' with us?"

Joel hesitated. Should he take the safer trail and leave with Smokey and Perkins? Or — he shook his head. "Jeff told me a lot about the Lazy F. I'm hankering to meet

139

this Samuel Fairfax. Once I do . . ." He shrugged.

"Whaat?" For the third time, Joel's coolness shocked Hayes. "You think bein' a preacher's goin' to save your skin? Better get out while you can."

"You just gave me the best protection of all," Joel defied him. "Now, if anything such as an unexpected accident happens to me, Perkins, Travis, and the rest of the men will have to swear they heard you threaten my life." He strode back to Querida, calmly mounted her, and rode back to the others.

Hayes changed his tune instantly. Greed etched itself on his face and in his eyes at the sight of the black mare. "Maybe I was hasty," he half apologized. "I didn't mean anythin'." He cleared his throat with an obvious effort. "Where'd a preacher get a horse like that?" His quivering forefinger pointed straight at Querida.

"I sure didn't steal her," Joel sarcastically told him.

Smokey and Perkins went off into convulsions of laughter. Hayes glared at them but pressed his lips tight before saying, "Looks like you came a long way."

Something in his inscrutable eyes blocked Joel from frankly admitting his journey and the reason for it as he had done at other ranches. His years among rough men had not been in vain; they had given him insight into human nature. Now, he weighed Hayes and found him wanting: mean enough to be dangerous but a coward at heart. The kind of bad man without the nerve to be thoroughly bad. Followed by rustlers but never respected. Ruthless but more likely to shoot a man from ambush than meet him in a fair fight, evidenced by the way he had framed Smokey Travis on some flimsy charge, then rushed through a hanging to rid himself of a trouble spot.

"Hayes, I'm riding up to the ranch house with Travis and Perkins so they can get their gear from the bunkhouse without any interference." He lowered his voice. "I wouldn't be too anxious about following close behind if I were you." His gaze included the rest of the riders. His sunny smile flashed. "On the other hand, I guess we don't have to worry about it, do we? Smokey's horse took off for parts unknown, so he'll have to borrow yours." He thought Hayes would explode before Smokey vaulted to the saddle of Hayes's horse and rode out of sight, closely followed by Perkins and Joel.

Hidden by the willow thicket and a stand of close-growing cottonwoods, Smokey reined in Hayes's horse and motioned for his comrades to stop. His dark eyes danced, and he said in a low voice, "I'm a mighty curious galoot, an' I bet if a feller or fellers were to creep back up on them rustlers, why, it just could be interesting."

Joel slid to the ground and tossed Querida's reins to Perkins. Smokey followed suit. "Keep the horses quiet," Joel ordered.

Disappointment filled Perkins's face. "Aw, why can't I go, too?"

"We may need those horses in a hurry," Joel replied. "If you hear us yell, come running." He ignored Perkins's grunt and followed Smokey's stocky frame back to the willow thicket. A few rods away, they took cover, close enough to hear but far enough away to avoid being seen. Smokey pressed Joel's hand for silence when the crashing of brush and curses nearby told them the men were retrieving their guns.

"I'll get Travis and Perkins and that goldy-haired rider who says he's a preacher." Hayes's furious voice came clearly. Joel felt a thrill go up his spine. Without hesitation or thought of the consequences, he had rushed in to save Smokey. Now, he would have to face the consequences.

"While you're at it, I bet you'll get your hands on that black mare, too, huh, Hayes? I seen how ya looked at her."

A start went through Joel's tall frame, and only Smokey's powerful hand dragging him back down kept the sometimes reckless young minister from betraying their hiding place.

Hayes's unpleasant laugh sawed its way into Joel's brain, and his words beat red-hot and searing. "The way I see it, a dead man don't need a horse."

A burst of raucous, threatening laughter followed, then the scrambling in the brush ceased. After an altercation on who would ride double, a lot of grumbling, and Hayes's loud remarks on the subject, the steady cadence of hoofbeats faded and died in the distance.

"Thought we were goners there for a minute." Smokey sat up. "Preacher, you've gotta learn to lie still when there's danger around, no matter what." He stood, offered a hand to Joel, and sternly added, "What's your handle, anyway? Jim — that's Perkins — an' me can't keep calling you Preacher."

"I wouldn't want you to." Joel brushed leaves from his clothes, and they retraced their steps to Jim and the horses. "My name's Joel. Uh, what will Hayes do now?"

"Make up some story on why he fired the Lazy F's two best hands," Jim put in sourly. He clamped a worn Stetson down on straggling brown locks.

"Let's beat him to it." Joel bit his tongue to keep from laughing at the amazement in the cowboys' faces.

"What'd ya say?" Perkins demanded, face reddening.

"Here's what we'll do," Joel said. "The way I figure it, after what happened, Hayes won't head straight for the ranch. Instead, he and his men will circle and come in later from another direction. He'll count on us being gone by the time he gets there. According to what you and Jeff said, whatever reason Hayes gives for firing you two will be swallowed whole by Fairfax." He drew his brows together. "Wonder why a man smart enough to own a spread like this doesn't have enough savvy to see through Hayes?"

"He plumb don't want to," the loquacious Jim put in. "I ain't talked much with Smokey about it, but even in the short time I've been here, it 'pears Hayes has some hold on the boss."

"Any idea what it is?" Joel mounted Querida, waited until Smokey clambered aboard Hayes's horse, and started up the trail.

"Not eggzackly, but I'm workin' on it." Jim suddenly clammed up, as if realizing how freely he'd talked to a stranger.

"What . . . uh . . . what's a preacher doing riding around in eastern New Mexico?" Smokey asked with a keen sidelong glance.

Joel deliberated for a full minute, then laid his cards on the table. "I'm looking for a man. I heard that Samuel Fairfax had been in these parts for a lot of years. Thought maybe he would have known of or have heard of my man."

"He might at that," Smokey said ponderously. "Did this feller do you wrong?"

"He doesn't even know I exist." A feeling stronger than himself prompted Joel to tell his story in a few brief sentences.

Jim, the more talkative of the two, spoke first. "That's the most peculiar tale I ever heard." He shook his head. "I never knew any Cyrus Scott." He scratched his cheek. "Never heard the name Cyrus, even."

"Smokey?"

"Naw. Beats me why you want to find your daddy, seeing he never knew you were born an' all that." He sounded doubtful.

"If he's still alive, I can't let him die without knowing about the Lord and that he's forgiven," Joel murmured.

A new constraint fell between them, broken only when Smokey pointed to the ground at a fork in the trail. "You predicted

145

right. Hayes and the men are heading away from the ranch house." A grin split his likable face. "Whoopee! This is gonna be fun." He goaded his horse into a gallop. "Race you to the corral."

Jim followed with a yell. Querida, trained to be in front in any race, leaped forward and stretched out full length until she became a flowing machine that ate up the trail in enormous gulps. She flashed past Jim, overtook Smokey in spite of his lead, and pounded ahead of the others until Joel took pity on them and slowed her so they could catch up. Then, he leaned forward, called into her ear, "Go, Querida!" and she put on a burst of speed that brought her to the Lazy F ranch house and corral in time for Joel to slide off her back and perch on the top rail of the fence until Smokey and Jim arrived.

"Snappin' crocodiles, if Hayes ever sees that mare run, your life won't be worth a dead cactus," Jim panted, admiration written all over him.

"She doesn't even look winded," Smokey complained after keenly observing Querida contentedly munching grass, reins over her head.

A trill of laughter, sweeter than the song of a meadowlark, broke into their conversa-

146

tion. Joel glanced toward the ranch house about a hundred yards from the corral where he sat. A slender, running figure had covered about half the distance. Joel had seen Indian girls run with the same fleet grace. He jumped down from the fence, bared his head, and waited for the girl, who could only be Rebecca Fairfax.

Clad in boys' jeans, a blue blouse, and red kerchief, her riding boots barely touched the ground. What little hair he could see from under her sombrero curled nut brown, almost the same shade as her merry eyes. Red lips parted over even, white teeth. "Smokey Travis, whose horse — why, it's Hayes's!" Blank astonishment obliterated her smile. She raced straight to the three men, then on to Querida. "Oh, you beauty!" She whirled. Fear replaced her natural joyousness. "Jim, Smokey, what — ?" A slim, tanned hand went to her throat, and her cheeks paled until the wild roses faded.

"Aw, it's nothing," Smokey mumbled.

"Don't lie to me." The brown eyes sparkled dangerously.

"Miss Fairfax?" Joel courteously began. "Is your father home?"

"Why, yes," she faltered. The fear in her eyes intensified.

"May we see him?"

"Of course, but —" She trotted alongside the men toward the ranch house.

"We'll explain everything," Joel reassured her. Some of the girl's trouble melted, and he heard her sigh of relief.

The quartet finished the walk to the large, porched, log home in silence. Joel noted the "H" shape, different from most ranch houses. They reached the bottom step, with Rebecca in the lead. The massive front door burst open. A tall man with graying brown hair and cold blue eyes stepped onto the porch. He fastened his gaze on Rebecca. "Didn't I tell you to keep away from the hands?"

"Father, something's wrong. Smokey came home riding Hayes's horse, chasing this stranger."

Joel could have sworn a look of actual relief brightened the intense blue eyes. Samuel Fairfax ignored his daughter's stumbling explanation and turned toward Joel. His mouth dropped open. He took a backward step as if hit by a battering ram.

Joel's heart leaped. This man must have somewhere encountered Cyrus! From babyhood, Judith and Gideon told him he was a replica of his father. Consternation brought Joel's spirits to earth with a resounding thud. Some tragedy lay between Samuel and

148

the long-missing Cyrus. Could they have met, quarreled, and settled their differences in the time-honored western tradition that added bodies to Boot Hills throughout the land? It could account for Hayes's stranglehold on Fairfax. If he knew . . .

Joel's imagination ran riot.

"Who are you, and what do you want?" Fairfax demanded.

Face-to-face with a possible end to his long search, Joel could not speak. Jim Perkins mercifully introduced him.

"Boss, this here's Joel Scott, and if he hadn't come ridin' in at just the right minute, well, ol' Smokey here'd be pushin' up the daisies."

"What's that?" Fairfax roared and turned his full attention to Perkins. Yet, the pallor of his first sight of Joel remained.

"Hayes rigged up some phony evidence to show Smokey was rustlin'," Jim explained. "Even fooled me. Wasn't even goin' to let Smokey speak up in his own defense, just roped him and got ready to hang him." Memory of the tense moments brought his story alive. "Hayes slapped Smokey's horse and left Smokey danglin', but quicker than a roadrunner, Scott steps out from a willow thicket, hauls out his guns, and cuts the rope with the best shootin' I ever saw. Then he up and covers us, makes Hayes crawl, finished the party by tellin' us he's a preacher, and beats Smokey and me in a race home ridin' that black mare over there."

Fairfax ignored Jim's pointing finger, his daughter's quick gasp of horror. "Travis, if Hayes says you were rustling, you were. Now get out of here. You're fired. You, too, Perkins."

"Too late, Boss," Jim said cheerfully. "Hayes done did that. We just rode in to get our gear and 'cause Scott here said you had the right to hear what really happened 'fore Hayes comes in with his lies."

Joel grinned at his audacity but not for long. Fairfax turned back to him, accusingly. "If you're some kind of preacher, why aren't you doing your job instead of sticking your nose in where it ain't wanted?"

"I'm looking for a man," Joel said for the second time that day. "Have you ever heard the name Cyrus Scott?"

"Kin of yours?"

"My father." Joel had difficulty forming the words.

Samuel Fairfax crossed his strong arms and stared. The logs of the ranch house behind him looked no stronger than their owner. "Why come sniveling to me? What did he do . . . this . . . what's his name? Oh yes, Cyrus Scott." His face turned even stonier.

"He married my mother using his brother's name, ran out on her before she found out she would bear his child, then fled from Texas when he learned of her death." Joel did not budge an inch.

"All that?" A sardonic smile accompanied his question. "Doesn't seem to me that you or anyone would chase around trying to find a man who'd do those things."

Joel took in a deep breath, held it, then let it go before he said, "If he's dead, I want to know it. If he isn't, he needs to know he's forgiven by God and his family." Truth rang in his voice. He saw something flicker in the cold eyes and added, "So is the man who killed him, if Father died by violence. God's love covers even that."

For a moment, Samuel Fairfax stood rigid. For an eternity, he stared into Joel's eyes. Smokey coughed, and the spell broke. Fairfax unfolded his arms and said, "If this Cyrus Scott is as foolhardy as his son, he probably died years ago." His boot heel ground into the porch when he turned and went back into the house. But before he closed the door, he called, "The best thing you can do is ride out with Travis and

151

Perkins. There's nothing on the Lazy F for you."

Was his glance at Rebecca, followed by a meaningful look back at Joel, meant as a deliberate warning? His mouth tasting like ashes, the young minister watched the door close. Its slamming sounded a death knell to his search — and his hopes.

CHAPTER 9

"Mr. Scott, I apologize for Father." A strong but shapely hand lightly touched Joel's arm and released him from his stupor.

He looked into Rebecca Fairfax's upturned face, dusky red from her efforts not to cry. Something in her troubled brown eyes reached out to him. Joel inhaled sharply; his humiliation at the hands of her father vanished. For some insane reason, he wanted to shout, to listen to his pumping heart instead of the common sense that told him to leave. He glanced at the hand still resting on his sleeve. *What would it be like to take that hand . . . and its owner . . . and ride away?*

Joel felt the blood rush to his head at the preposterous idea. He had known Rebecca Fairfax less than an hour. He ignored the little voice inside that demanded, *So what?* "It's all right, Miss Fairfax." He looked deep into her lovely eyes. "We'll meet again."

153

The assurance in his words set new red flags waving in Rebecca's face. "I . . . I don't see how," she faltered.

Smokey Travis and Jim Perkins had been standing silent during Joel's altercation with the owner of the Lazy F. Now, they stepped forward, Stetsons in hand. Smokey half closed his keen dark eyes and drawled, "A preacher preaches, doesn't he? If I know Samuel Fairfax, an' I do, even he won't kick up a dust storm 'cause his daughter wants to go to a meeting."

"That's how I see it, too," Jim eagerly assented, his boyish face opening into a wide grin. "Pards, we'd better get out of here." He pointed to a distant band of dark riders heading toward the ranch house. Pure devilment shone in his eyes. "But we could pervide a welcomin' committee."

"You'd better go," Rebecca told them. A shadow swept over her sweet face. "Smokey, thanks for being my friend. Good luck, Jim." But her gaze fastened on Joel. "Goodbye, Mr. Scott. God help you in your search for your father." She stepped back.

"Will you be all right?" Joel hurriedly added, "Hayes is going to be in a nasty mood."

"God and Mrs. Cook, our cook, will look after me!" Her red lips twitched. "The worst

154

Father can do is send me to my room."

"An' your window's big enough for ya to climb out if ya had to," Perkins observed.

Rebecca looked startled at the thought, then nodded.

Five minutes later, Joel on Querida, Smokey on the buckskin that had come straight back to the ranch, and Jim on a trim pinto that he said was his rode away. Rebecca waved good-bye to them from the ranch house porch.

"Kinda hate leavin' her here to face Hayes," Jim growled.

"She'll be all right. I used to think someday I'd up an' marry her," Smokey said somberly. "Get her away from Hayes."

"Why didn't you?" Joel could not keep the words back, but when Smokey's face darkened, he wished he had kept still.

"Rebecca thinks a whole lot of me, but it's like the brother she never had but should have." Smokey stared ahead at the path wide enough for them to ride three abreast. "At least I was her friend, as much as Hayes and Fairfax allowed." He turned toward Joel. "I never was good enough for her. Perkins here or the other hands aren't, either. Now, a strapping young feller like you might just —" He never finished what he started to say. His buckskin chose that moment to shy away from some real or imagined danger and execute a dance that kept Smokey busy and Joel and Jim laughing at the horse's antics.

But the young minister did not forget the gleam in Smokey's eyes. If he could win the cowboy's confidence, he would have a loyal friend for life. The same held true with Perkins, witnessed to by the way he stood up to Hayes back by the willow thicket.

"I need supplies." Joel shoved aside meditations and spoke. "I suppose I can get what I need at the Mexican village?" He intercepted the quick glance Jim sent Smokey, the lifting of eyebrows before Jim drawled, "We've seen ya ride and shoot. Can you rope?"

"A little." Joel stifled a grin, glanced around, and selected a cottonwood stump off to their left. He uncoiled his lariat from the saddle horn, swung it in a wide loop, and dropped it over the stump with an expert twist of his wrist.

"Yup, ya can rope . . . a little." Perkins waited until Joel twitched the lasso, recoiled it, and put it back in place. "Why don't you 'n' me 'n' Smokey get jobs t'gether? Like the fellers in that book."

"The Three Musketeers?" Joel's heart lifted at the thought, and a pang of lonesomeness for his comrades back on the Double J went through him. "Think anyone will hire a preacher?"

"Sure, if you're with us. Right, Smokey?"

"Haw, haw!" Smokey grabbed his hat and slapped it against his leg. His horse went into another spin.

"What's so funny, ya bowlegged galoot?" Perkins demanded as soon as Smokey got the buckskin quieted.

Tears of laughter streaming down his dark face, Smokey choked, "I reckon any rancher who sees what our new pard can do won't worry about him preaching on his own time." He wiped his eyes with a bright neckerchief. "Say, Joel, how about playing a joke on the Bar Triangle? That's the next biggest spread to the Lazy F an' always wanting good riders."

"What kind of joke?" Joel looked at Smokey suspiciously.

"We'll ride in, ask for jobs, an' not let on you're a preacher."

"Naw," Jim chimed in. "That ain't no good. When they find out, they'll think Joel's ashamed of it."

Smokey's jaw dropped. "I never thought about that." He ruefully shook his head. A moment later, his dark eyes twinkled again. "Well, how about just not telling how fast

157

his mare is?"

Jim sat up straighter; mischief filled his lean face. "Then, when the Mexican village holds their fiesta day, Joel c'n enter his horse — what's her handle, anyhow?"

"Querida. Spanish for *beloved.*"

"Kayreeda'll purely outrun ev'ry horse in New Mexico," Jim predicted.

"Not Vermilion." Smokey glared at Perkins.

Jim snorted. "Think old man Fairfax'll let Rebecca ride in any race? Not 'til all the dogies come home wearin' ribbons in their ears." He rolled his eyes.

Joel, the peacemaker, asked, "What kind of horse is Vermilion? I've yet to see an animal beat Querida, given an equal start."

"He's the purtiest, best-tamed, brightest-red mustang you ever saw," Jim admitted. "Smokey caught him an' babied him an' gave him to Rebecca on her eighteenth birthday last December." He pushed his Stetson farther back on his head. "Smokey, I'd lay even odds on Vermilion an' the black."

Smokey jealously eyed the beautiful mare. "She might win a short race, but Vermilion can't be beat in a long one."

Joel smothered a grin. The longer the race, the better Querida performed. "No sense arguing about it. When does this fiesta day come off, anyway?"

"After roundup. The whole country comes."

"Who won the horse race last year?" Joel inquired.

"Hayes." The corners of Smokey's mouth turned down. "His big bay's a grand horse." He laughed gleefully. "I did enjoy riding him today. He ain't no match for your horse or Vermilion, though. Is it a deal? We keep mum an' surprise folks at the race?"

"Why not? We won't be lying or anything."

"I wouldn't ask a preacher to lie." Smokey sent his buckskin into a run and left Joel staring after him.

"Did I say something wrong?" asked Joel.

"Don't pay no 'tention to Smokey," Jim advised. "He's taken a shine to ya, but sometimes he's plum' peecooliar about things. Love does that to some fellers." Jim shook his head and looked wise.

"Do you have a girl?" Joel asked curiously.

Perkins's blinding smile burst forth again. "Sure. Conchita's the most beautiful gal in the Mexican village. Soon's I save a little money, I'm gonna hawg-tie her an' marry her before some long-legged jasper beats me to it." A thundercloud drove away his sunny look. "An' if Hayes don't quit hangin'

159

around her all the while he's playin' up to Fairfax, intendin' to marry Rebecca, there's gonna be trouble like you never saw."

A cold breeze of foreboding blew across Joel's heart. "You mean that rustler's actually —"

Jim nodded and looked far older than his young years. They had nearly caught up with Smokey and the buckskin, who waited for them where the road forked. "Don't say nothin' in front of Smokey," Jim cautioned in a whisper. "He hates Hayes the polecat enough already."

If ever a range were white and needing harvest for God, this wild New Mexico land fit the description! Joel silently followed his new friends. Miles later, the Bar Triangle cattle with their distinctive brand replaced the herds of Lazy F stock.

With his first view of the Bar Triangle house and outbuildings, Joel's heart beat faster. Unlike the Lazy F, the original Bar Triangle owners had built of adobe. In many ways, the main house reminded Joel of his grandparents' hacienda. Low, long, and cool, the splashing fountain in the courtyard merrily welcomed the dusty, tired riders. The owner, Ben Lundeen, practically greeted them with open arms.

"Travis, Perkins, I figured someday you'd

come riding in looking for work. It's a wonder you lasted so long as you did on the Lazy F, 'specially you, Smokey. Everyone knows Fairfax don't cotton to younger riders." His firm grip and keen look measured Joel. "Who's your pard?"

"Joel Scott, an all-round ridin', ropin', shootin' hand, plus he's a preacher," the irrepressible Jim bragged.

"Whaat?" Lundeen's eyes bulged in his strong face. Doubt crept into his voice. "I don't know about hiring a preacher. What'll the men say?"

Quick-witted as a ground squirrel in danger, Joel replied, "Why not let them decide? Put me on for a week, then ask your outfit if they want me to stay." He glanced away from Lundeen long enough to catch Smokey's delighted grin and the way Perkins put one hand over his mouth.

"Fair enough." Lundeen nodded. "You boys know where the bunkhouse is. Go stow your gear." His eyes gleamed, and he casually added, "You can do as you like about telling the men about your interrupted necktie party."

"How'd you know?" Jim belligerently placed both hands on his hips in a fighting stance.

Again, that curious gleam filled Lundeen's

161

eyes. "You'll find an old friend in the cook-house. He rode in earlier today with an interesting tale for my ears only. Said he couldn't stand living with the kind of men Hayes has been hiring and that he reckoned the only two worth much wouldn't be staying."

"So, you knew all the time we were coming!" Chagrin fell on Smokey's expressive face.

"I didn't know young Scott was a preacher," Lundeen admitted. "I guess that little fact got by Curly. He spilled the other to me, and I told him to keep quiet." Trouble brooded on the lined face. "The men will hear of it soon enough. You know range talk." His gaze bored into his new riders. "It's up to Scott to prove himself."

"He will," Smokey predicted.

"Yeah, but if anythin' happens an' Joel don't stay, we go, too," Jim loyally added.

"Fair enough." Lundeen's rare smile lightened his countenance, and he looked years younger. "Go get settled." He wandered down toward the corral with them to where they had tied their horses. His steps quickened, and he headed straight for Querida. "Whose mare is this?" He stroked her soft nose.

"Mine." Pride of ownership and the long,

faithful trail they had ridden together underlined the word.

"She's a beauty. You wouldn't want to sell her."

"No."

"I wouldn't, either, if I owned her." He patted Querida again, and his eyes flashed. "Good thing you're here instead of on some of the ranches. Your horse is safe on the Bar Triangle." His unspoken words, *but not on the Lazy F,* hung in the quiet air until Lundeen said, "Tomorrow we'll see what you can do, Scott," and trailed back up to his house.

It took less than a week for the Bar Triangle crew to accept Joel Scott. His range skills showed up with the best and won the respect of both men his age and much older. Lundeen just grunted at Joel's display of hard work and expertise.

True to their pact, Jim, Smokey, and Joel did not breathe a word about Querida's fleetness, even when some of the hands said a trifle too nonchalantly, "Bet she can run. Are you going to ride her in the fiesta race?"

"I might." Joel lounged on his bunk, as he had done dozens of times on the Double J. In spite of being the adopted son-of-the-house, once he had learned to ride with the outfit, he spent a lot of time in the bunk-house and kept a bedroll there.

"Sure will be some race," some of the boys sighed enviously. "Sure hope Hayes don't win again. He wouldn't, if Fairfax'd let that girl of his ride her red horse," seemed to be the general agreed-on opinion.

"Once, when I was separatin' our cattle from the Lazy F's, I saw her racin' across the range," one cowboy said. "Never will forget it. She rode just like an Indian, bent forward in the saddle 'til her and that Vermilion looked like one critter."

"Hey, Travis, how come Fairfax's so all-fired anxious to get her hitched up with Hayes?" someone called out.

Smokey's pupils dwindled to pinpoints of blackness. "Crazy, I reckon." He breathed hard. "Beats me."

A frank-faced, young rider confessed, "I'da got me a job there in hopes of some-times seein' the girl, but, even for that, I couldn't stomach Hayes. One of these times, he's gonna get his." Cold steel rang beneath the idle words.

Joel spent Sunday afternoon propped against an ancient oak, considering his future. He knew he had passed his trial at the Bar Triangle; he also felt at home. Yet, how could range work be related to his two missions: finding his father and preaching? A burst of song from the bunkhouse brought a sympathetic smile to his carved lips. Jim must be getting duded up to go call on Conchita. On impulse, Joel left his tree friend and ambled back to the bunkhouse. "Perkins, mind if I ride to the Mexican village with you?"

"Not atall." Jim's face was flushed with the efforts of pulling on boots shined almost as brightly as his eyes. His Sunday-white shirt and colorful scarf pleasantly added to his excited, handsome face. "Just don't ya get no ideas about her."

"I won't," Joel promised and turned to Smokey. "Are you coming?"

His friend looked up from a magazine he was reading, disgust etched into his face. "Might as well." He threw the magazine aside, stood, and stretched. "The feller who wrote the story I was reading has never been west of Boston! According to him, all us cowboys sleep in our chaps an' don't eat nothing but beef an' beans. Too bad he doesn't come out here for a spell an' see the meals Curly turns out for us poor, miserable punchers."

"Better of him if he don't come," Jim said sagely. "It'd be too bad if a feller like that got the outfit turned loose on him."

165

Joel laughed, but on the way to the village, he asked, "Do you think some of the men would come if I found a place to preach some Sunday?"

"They might," Smokey said after a sidelong look at Jim that Joel duly noted. "There's a padre in the Mexican village an' a little church, but not many of the ranchers go to Mass an' none of the hands." He pondered for a minute. "Now that we're on permanent-like at the Bar Triangle, ask Lundeen if it would be all right to hold a meeting there. He's honest all the way through; so's his wife. Kids are all grown and gone."

"Good idea," Jim seconded. "Maybe Rebecca Fairfax would ride over an' you could see her . . . horse Vermilion."

Joel knew exactly what Jim hinted and could not keep color from rising until he sarcastically thought, *I must be the same shade as the wonder horse they keep praising.* It made him feel hotter than ever.

"You better forget her an' keep your mind on Conchita," Smokey told him. "If you don't marry her pretty soon, I'll up an' beat you."

"She wouldn't look at the likes of ya," Jim loftily told his partner.

"Why not? I'm better looking than some

166

people around here," Smokey retorted. "Even if I don't have a brand-new shirt an' a kerchief I could use to scare off a wild bull."

They good-naturedly wrangled all the way to the Mexican village, heaping mock insults on each other and appealing to Joel for support, and looking disgusted when he would not take sides.

The Mexican village resembled similar ones he had seen in his travels. Adobe buildings, strings of red and green peppers, the tang of dust and horseflesh, guitar music from a cantina, laughter, and the after-siesta relaxation of a Sunday.

"Conchita lives with her married sister," Jim explained when they stopped before a cream building with the inevitable red-tiled roof. Green vines grew up and over, giving an illusion of coolness Joel knew would be present even on the hottest day.

The door stood open. They dismounted and hitched their horses to a crude rail fence. Perkins's spurs jingled musically when he led the way up a path made of flat stones.

"Pard, ain't that Hayes's bay?" Smokey crouched and pointed toward a tethered horse grazing nearby, barely visible through a clump of cottonwoods.

Jim stopped in midstride. His face whitened, then a look that sent fear crawling through Joel spread across Jim's face. In the frozen second before Perkins leaped for the open doorway, a low cry came from inside the house.

Like a speeding bullet, Jim bounded inside. Smokey and Joel raced after him. The trio burst through an empty room toward the sound of a voice that pleaded, "No, no, Señor!"

"That dirty scoundrel!" Smokey choked. He and Joel crowded through the door to the small courtyard until they stood side by side with Perkins. A man with mousy brown hair stood with his back to them. An ashen-faced Mexican girl, whose disheveled dark hair and terrified eyes told the whole story, struggled in the man's arms. A ruffled white blouse sagged over one brown shoulder, and the red rose in her hair drooped in bizarre contrast to her distorted face. Hayes's fingers dug into her soft arms, and he jerked her closer. She screamed.

"Hayes!" Perkins's low, deadly voice loosened the man's hold. Hayes reached for his gun and whirled. Revolver half out of his holster, the livid-faced man faced the three men. He stared straight into Perkins's face — and saw death from the steady Colt

168

covering him, the trigger being slowly squeezed.

CHAPTER 10

Horror so deep he could neither pray nor move engulfed Joel. Then, Smokey struck up Perkins's gun with one hand, while keeping Hayes covered with the Colt in his other. Perkins's shot fired harmlessly into the ceiling.

"Drop it, Hayes!" Smokey ordered.

Hayes's revolver clattered to the floor. His mouth worked helplessly; rage and wonder mingled. Long scratches on his cheeks oozed blood. He finally burst out, "You!"

"Why'd ya do it?" Jim Perkins cried. Anger still mottled his face. "The dirty skunk don't deserve to live an' ya know it! Why didn't ya let me kill him?"

Joel shrank from Smokey's bitter laugh. "Think I did it for him? Naw. He ain't worth spilling blood for." He laughed again, a wild sound that turned Hayes's face even grayer. "Besides, someday he's going to hang." He waved toward the door with his

170

gun. "Get out, Hayes, an' don't come back here — ever. I reckon I saved your life; now I'm telling you, the next time . . ." He choked, and his dark eyes glittered.

Hayes did not say a word. He stumbled past Joel, who stepped aside from the doorway and let him go through.

Joel was sickened by the violent scene he had just witnessed, a scene that nearly led to death. His ears rang, and a few moments later, he heard hoof-beats, and he knew Hayes had fled.

"Conchita, are you all right?" The Jim who knelt by the girl bore little resemblance to the cowboy who, but for Smokey's interference, would have killed Conchita's attacker.

"Yes." She pulled her blouse back onto her shoulder. Great drops made her black eyes look like twin lakes at midnight under New Mexican stars. "He come, grab me. I fight." She extended broken-nailed hands that still trembled. "Hayes is bad." Conchita leaned against Jim.

Smokey jerked his head toward the doorway and walked out. Joel followed, conscious of shame. Not only for men like Hayes, who sank so low they made girls' and women's lives on the frontier a nightmare but for his own inadequacies. He, a minister of God, had stood speechless and powerless in the face of peril. Thank God Smokey had not.

Humbled by his lack of ability to act when necessary, a shortcoming Joel had not known he possessed, he hoarsely told his new friend, "It's a good thing you were here." He shuddered; drops of sweat sprang to his forehead. "Hayes can't help being grateful that you . . . after what he tried to do . . ."

Smokey's look of contempt stopped his stuttering. "Like I said, it wasn't for Hayes. I just couldn't stand for Jim to have a killing on his head. It would always be between him an' Conchita, for one thing. For another, Hayes's time is getting short on this range. That Lone Man Canyon business shows that." An unpleasant smile twisted his lips. He glanced back at the house, then at all sides of the wide porch where they had stopped to wait for Jim. "You look like a feller who could keep things under his hat."

"I am." Joel braced himself for the startling revelation he felt coming.

Smokey again checked to make sure they were not observed before he pulled back his vest just far enough for Joel to catch a flash of silver.

"Smokey Travis, you're a —"

"Shh. Don't tell Jim," the shorter man warned in a whisper when heavy footfalls and lighter steps announced Perkins and Conchita's arrival.

Perkins's arm lay protectively around her waist. Tearstains could not disguise the Mexican girl's beauty. Her eyes glowed with happiness that reflected in her sweetheart's face. "Joel, you're a preacher. Will ya marry us?"

Jim's question drove the thought of the deputy marshal's badge that Smokey wore clean out of Joel's head. "Why, yes," he stammered. "But —"

"Pard, how can you get married?" Smokey demanded. "Where are you going to take Conchita if you do?"

A look of doubt did not change Jim's dogged determination. "We'll ride out an' find a job somewhere. Connie's willin' to work at cleanin' or cookin'." His mouth tightened. "Snappin' crocodiles, Smokey, ya don't expect me to leave her here, do ya?"

Smokey pondered. "It ain't none of my business, but if it were me, why, I'd just pack up Conchita an' her duds an' take her back to the Bar Triangle with us." A smile, singular in its sweetness, crept to his face. "Mrs. Lundeen'll take care of her 'til you get a place, especially when she hears what

173

Hayes tried to do."

"Connie, will ya trust me an' my pards an' go?" Jim's poignant question set Joel's heart to pounding. So did the love in Conchita's liquid eyes when she said, "Yes," and pressed her face against Perkins's still-fresh white shirt. She raised her head, smiled mistily at Joel and Smokey, and ran lightly back inside.

Smokey, the coolest of the three, snickered and asked, "Do you have any money?"

"Money?" Jim stared at him.

"Yeah. Pesos, cartwheels, simoleons, good old American dollars."

"Not much." Jim spread out a pitiful array and turned deep red. "Uh, what do I need money for?"

Smokey threw his hands up in exasperation. "How're you going to get Conchita to the ranch? Does she have a horse?"

Joel laughed out loud at the comical look on Jim's bewildered face. "Don't worry. I've got plenty." He laughed again when his comrades gasped at the bills he pulled from his shirt. "Buy her a horse, Jim. Get a pack mule if you need it."

"I can't take your money," he protested.

"Call it a wedding present."

"Whoopee!" Smokey yelled. Jim rushed back inside. He returned wearing the grin

Joel had come to associate with his light-hearted companion. "Connie says she doesn't need a pack mule. All she has is her clothes an' we can stow them in our saddle-bags." His eyes glinted when he awkwardly added, "Thanks . . . both of ya." His face reddened. "I'm just glad we got here when we did."

"Thank God for that," Joel soberly agreed. "Wonder how Hayes is going to explain to Fairfax what happened? The Lazy F's bound to hear range gossip."

Smokey fixed a warning gaze on Joel. "You can bet your life that snake'll come up with lies enough to make himself out an angel an' the rest of us devils," he darkly prophesied. Conchita peeked out the door, and by unspoken consent, they dropped the subject. Just before dusk, the three men and a tired Conchita, unused to hours in the saddle, dismounted at the Bar Triangle.

"Pards, come with us," Jim begged. They nodded and trailed Jim and his drooping bride-to-be inside the adobe ranch house.

If Joel had ever entertained qualms about Perkins's sincerity, they vanished when Jim manfully told the surprised Lundeens, "Conchita and me aim to get married soon as I can fix a place for her. My pards and me got to her place today just in time to

175

save her from Hayes." His eyes flashed. "Smokey said he thought you could look after her. She's willin' to work hard."

Not by a flicker of an eyelash did either Ben Lundeen or his kindly wife betray shock. Mrs. Lundeen stood, took both of Conchita's hands in her own, and said in a genteel voice, "How nice to have a girl with us again! Now that our daughter's gone, I just get hungry for another woman's company." She smiled and added, "Come, Conchita. You'll want to freshen up from your long ride."

Joel's eyes stung. The woman's acceptance and unfailing hospitality reminded him of Judith; so would she have taken in a stray.

Lundeen waited until the ladies disappeared, then inquired, "How's Hayes?"

Joel shuddered at the implication. Womenfolk in the West were to be protected and those who transgressed, punished. *God, will the day ever come when law and order other than the law of retribution rule this land?*

"Hayes'll think twice before he gets in our way again," Smokey slowly told Lundeen. His eyes shone like molten metal. "That's the second time our paths have crossed."

Joel silently added, *I pray to God there won't be another.*

■ ■ ■ ■

During the days that Joel proved himself at the Bar Triangle and settled into the outfit, Rebecca Fairfax had troubles of her own. A strange restlessness filled her, stemming from the two different versions of the attempted hanging of Smokey Travis.

Samuel made sure his daughter was present when Hayes rode in with his story of catching Smokey in the act of rustling. She noticed how he downplayed the young minister's part in it. All he said was, "Fool stranger interfered, and the men and I let Travis go after firing him and that mouthy Perkins." Yet, the girl hugged to her heart the clean blue fire of Joel Scott's eyes, his waving corn silk hair, tanned skin, and, most of all, the look in his face when he quietly said they would meet again.

How? She considered the question from her favorite range viewpoints, in her bed at night. Other comments haunted her, including Jim Perkins's laconic observation about her window being large enough to climb through if she had to.

One tense day followed another. Her father grew more taciturn and unapproachable than ever. If it had not been for the faithful Mrs. Cook, Rebecca could not have stood it. More and more, she spent free time in the kitchen, one of her few refuges away from the ever-present Clyde Hayes, who had renewed his pursuit of her, no, intensified it. Sometimes, she felt she would eventually be forced to marry Hayes simply because her father commanded it.

Yet, every time she thought of it, she cried out, "Never!" She also began to heed Mrs. Cook's lessons about trusting in the Lord and asking for His protection and help. Verses in the Bible that Rebecca had not known existed now offered comfort.

Late one Sunday night, she and her father sat reading in the big living room, a rare occurrence. Usually, if he came in before dark, Samuel buried himself in papers concerning the ranch. Tonight, she stole glances at him from behind a well-worn copy of *The Pilgrim's Progress,* a book Mrs. Cook said would help Rebecca forget her own troubles. How old and worn he looked, as if life had effectively stamped out any happiness he had ever known.

Rebecca impulsively left her chair and went to stand before him. "Father, what is it? You seem so sad." He didn't speak for such a long time that she wondered if he had heard her. When he did speak, his words left her stunned.

"Rebecca, if you don't marry Clyde Hayes, I am ruined." He spread his hands wide, expressing defeat as she had never seen him do before. His eyes pleaded. "Daughter, will you save me?"

She almost fell to her knees and promised. Then the memory of Hayes laying hands on her stilled her voice. Marriage with him would be torment until death mercifully freed her. "Father, I —"

The door flew open and slammed back against the wall with a mighty bang. Clyde Hayes strode in, glowering. Red welts stood out on his pale face, and his colorless eyes flamed with triumph. Rebecca shrank away from him.

"Hayes? What happened to you? Looks like you tangled with a wildcat."

"Might as well have." He dropped heavily into a chair without being invited. "That's what a man gets for tryin' to help a woman he don't care about."

"What are you talking about?" Fairfax dropped the book he still held.

"I rode into the Mexican village. Found Travis and Perkins attackin' the girl called Conchita. I challenged them, and they vamoosed with their tails between their legs. They sneaked back up on me, and I pulled

179

my gun. Next thing I knew, the girl was all over me, scratchin' and spittin'. Last time I'll mix in."

Rebecca stared in disbelief. The part about Conchita scratching was obviously true. The rest she did not believe.

Neither did she believe it when Hayes contemptuously added, "That kid who calls himself a preacher was there, too. Didn't do any showin' off this time, though. Too scared, probably."

"It's an outrage when things like this go on right here on our range," Fairfax shouted. "I've a mind to get the outfit and ride down there myself." Rebecca noticed the fear in Hayes's face before he quickly said, "It ain't worth it. Besides, the girl's gone. I hid in a clump of cottonwood and watched them ride out. The men had scared up a horse for the girl, and the four of them rode off. I followed a spell, and they were headed for the Bar Triangle."

"Mighty strange they'd go that way." Samuel's eyebrows met in a frown. "The Lundeens and their ranch that's getting bigger all the time are a cactus spine in the leg, but they're decent folk. They won't put up with them."

Hayes glanced at Rebecca, whose heart nearly burst with indignation. "Oh, those men'll have some story," he carelessly said. "I just wanted you to hear what really happened."

She almost retorted, "If we want the truth, we won't get it from you," but bit her tongue and edged toward the door.

"Where are you goin'?" Hayes arrogantly demanded.

It took all Rebecca's control to say, "I rode a long way today, and I'm tired. Good night, Father, Mr. Hayes." She whipped out of the room and ran to her own.

Later, after she heard the front door close and knew Hayes had gone, she crept noiselessly down the hall and peered into the living room. Her father sat before the dying fire, graying brown head bowed as if in despair. Pity stirred her. A burning stick snapped; Samuel Fairfax groaned. Rebecca leaned forward and strained her ears to catch his low words. "God — is there no end to it?"

She wanted to go to him, but fear held her prisoner. If she did, he might ask her again to become the purchase price for his — what? Freedom? Life? Peace of mind? On hesitant feet, Rebecca stole back to her room, only to lie sleepless for hours and watch the mysterious night, shadowy and filled with uncertainty, just like her life.

Morning brought relief. No matter what, she could never marry Hayes. She avoided being alone with her father, unwilling to start another bitter argument. With Smokey no longer on the ranch to protect her, Rebecca sometimes felt herself to be a prisoner. She dared not ride far from home for fear of encountering Hayes. Not that she stood in awe of him. Vermilion could outrun Hayes's bay, and Rebecca could defend herself ably with her marksmanship. Yet, if she were forced to do so, would Father believe what she said or listen to Hayes? She could not risk finding out.

The morning after he rode in, Rebecca had privately told Hayes's story to Mrs. Cook. Her shrewd blue eyes and round face showed how little stock she put in anything Hayes said. "Looks to me like what probably happened was the other way around," she said and punched down the bread dough as if she had Hayes on the well-floured board. "If I know folks — and I do — neither Smokey nor young Perkins would have dishonorable intentions toward any girl. As for that young preacher, I only got a glimpse of him, but what I saw is in his favor."

A few days later, Mrs. Cook said, "Mrs.

Lundeen sent word over there'd be a meeting on Sunday at the Bar Triangle. She invited us to come Saturday and stay over. Want to go?" Her eyes sparkled. "It's been a long time since we had a visiting preacher come through."

"I don't suppose Father will consent," Rebecca said despondently, while her heart beat fast at the idea of an outing and the chance to see Joel Scott again.

"Let me ask him," Mrs. Cook suggested.

"All right, but it won't do any good."

Rebecca's pessimism held all that day but miraculously left at supper when Mrs. Cook said, "Mr. Fairfax, the Lundeens are holding a meeting on Sunday and asked us to come over Saturday and stay. I think we should go, all of us. Rebecca needs to be with folks other than us."

Samuel laid his fork down. "You do, do you?" He frowned.

"Yes, I do. It pays a body to let the neighbors know he's friendly."

Fairfax jerked at the word "he," took a mouthful of beefsteak, chewed it thoughtfully, and swallowed. "Might not be a bad idea. I've been meaning to talk to Lundeen about roundup. This is probably as good a time as any."

Mrs. Cook reverted to her humble servant

role. "Thank you, Sir." But, when she went to bring in the dessert, she lifted her eyebrows in a victory signal behind the master-of-the-house's back.

Rebecca could scarcely believe it. She wanted to mention the jaunt to her father but held her tongue. To do so might cause him to change his mind, and she simply had to go.

On Friday before the meeting, a second messenger arrived from the Bar Triangle. "There's gonna be a weddin' tomorrow night," he told Mrs. Cook and Rebecca. "Bring your fanciest clothes." He looked at the girl admiringly. "Uh, Smokey Travis sends greetin's."

"Is Smokey getting married?" Mrs. Cook gasped.

The rider shook his head. "Nope. It's that pard of his." He glanced at Rebecca again. "All the boys at the Bar Triangle are jealous. Lundeen's done fixed up a little cabin for the newlyweds." He grinned. "This is sure a big weekend for the preacher."

Before Rebecca could ask why, the rider shifted in the saddle. The girl followed his glance toward her father riding in.

"Gotta go. See y'all tomorrow." He spurred his horse and rode off with a cheerful wave and a tip of his hat to Fairfax.

"Who was that, and what did he want?" Samuel demanded sharply when he reached the house and slid from the saddle.

Mrs. Cook placidly said, "Mrs. Lundeen sent word we'd get in on a wedding as well as preaching and to bring our good clothes."

"Wedding? Whose?" The words shot like bullets out of Samuel's pinched mouth.

"Why, I don't rightly know, except it isn't Smokey Travis. Kind of sounded like it might be the young preacher himself."

Fairfax stared at her, dumbfounded. An odd look covered his face, one Rebecca had never before seen. "Scott? Who's the bride?"

"I don't know that, either," Mrs. Cook admitted. "Maybe one of the girls from the Mexican village."

Anger contorted Samuel's features. He brushed past the two women, slammed into the house, and let the door crash behind him.

"My stars," Mrs. Cook gasped. "What did I say to set him off? He sounded like he actually cared who the preacher married!"

He isn't the only one who cares, a wicked little voice inside Rebecca taunted. She raised her chin defiantly and said, "What does it matter? Come help me decide what to wear, will you, please?" Yet, all during the choosing of just the right gown and pressing and carefully packing it before the wedding, Rebecca's heart lay cold and heavy in her chest, making it hard for her to breathe and talk normally.

Chapter 11

One look into Conchita's innocent, dark eyes put to rest forever any suspicion Rebecca carried concerning the Mexican girl's reputation. An hour after the Lazy F contingent reached the Bar Triangle, the two maidens giggled and chattered as if they were long-separated sisters — especially when Conchita blushingly confessed she had been in love with "Señor Jeem" ever since young Perkins first visited the village.

Why should a great burden roll off Rebecca's shoulders? Her face rivaled the pink rose tucked in her nut-brown hair.

Later, Smokey managed to whisk Rebecca out of her father's vigilant scrutiny and whisper, "How come Hayes showed up? Did he trail you?"

Rebecca made a sound of disgust; a frown marred her pretty face. "I couldn't believe it when he said he reckoned he'd mosey along." Her eyes flashed. "I overheard

Father tell Hayes privately there had better not be any trouble."

"An' what did Hayes say to that?" Smokey's intense, dark gaze never left her face.

"He told Father he wouldn't start anything but if —" She hastily swallowed Hayes's derogatory "those three snakes" and substituted, "If anyone started trouble, he'd see that he finished it." She caught Smokey's rigid arm with one hand. "For Conchita's sake and mine, keep away from him."

"I can't back away if he comes looking for me," Smokey protested. Storm signals waved in his face. Rebecca could see he was torn between wanting to please her and following the range law that demanded a man answer an insult.

She lowered her voice. "It's just that every time Hayes gets mixed up in something, Father pushes me more to marry him. I can't, Smokey, I just can't. If only we could prove how rotten Hayes is and get him sent away!"

A curious expression rested on the cowboy's lean face. "Keep holding out. Maybe one of these days, we'll nail Hayes." He grinned, and mischief lurked in his eyes. "My new pard's been looking forward to seeing you again."

188

Rebecca could not stop the rich blush that mantled her face. "Oh? How strange, since Jim's marrying Conchita tonight."

"My other pard. The long-legged galoot duded up ready to perform the ceremony who's leaning against the door frame an' watching us." He raised one hand, motioned Joel to join them, and whispered in a woebegone voice, "Since you only care for me like a brother, you couldn't do better than Scott. He may be a preacher, but he's a real man, too. I sneaked around an' listened while he practiced preaching. He talks 'most as well as he rides an' ropes an' shoots."

"We meet again, Miss Fairfax. I'm glad." Joel's eyes glowed like blue jewels. In spite of obvious attempts to make his blond hair lie down, it lay in waves and looked even more golden in contrast with his suntanned skin. His blinding smile set Rebecca's heart to beating.

"It's nice to be here," she said noncommittally and held out her hand. It lost itself in Joel's strong one, but she noticed he made no effort to hold it longer than courtesy allowed, unlike some riders who used introductions as an excuse for extra friendliness.

"Excuse me, but I'd better hunt up Perkins an' make sure he hasn't got cold feet."

Smokey abruptly abandoned them. Rebecca found herself at a loss for words and felt horrified when she heard her own voice asking, "Mr. Scott, why did you and Smokey and Jim bring Conchita here?"

The blue gaze turned to steel. "No gentleman speaks to a lady of what would have happened to her if we hadn't arrived just when we did. Thank God we came."

His heartfelt prayer filled in all the blanks left by his refusal to discuss what she had suspected all along — that Hayes had been the villain.

A little later, Conchita confirmed it. While dressing in the beautiful white gown and Spanish lace mantilla Mrs. Lundeen had kindly lent her for her wedding, she told Rebecca in a few broken whispers how Hayes came, took her by surprise, and attacked her. "He is bad," she finished. "Señorita, never let him find you alone." It took all Rebecca could do to change the fear in the bride-to-be's eyes to the joy that rightfully belonged to her on her wedding day.

Conchita had shyly asked Rebecca to stand up with her, along with Smokey, who flanked the eager groom. Glad that she had heeded Mrs. Cook's advice not to wear white and rival the bride, Rebecca's rose pink gown swished around her ankles and made a perfect background for the dark-haired girl who turned toward Perkins in perfect trust. Quite a crowd of neighbors had ridden to the Bar Triangle for the event. Admiration of the young women's beauty rippled through the small crowd.

Rebecca could openly observe Joel throughout the simple but touching ceremony. His face shone with goodness. He spoke of the responsibility Jim and Conchita faced and the happiness they could find in one another by becoming part of God's plan for husbands and wives since time began. When he came to the question, "Do you, Conchita, take Jim . . . ," Rebecca thought, *What would it be like, promising to take a man for better and worse, in sickness and health; mutually agreeing to be his companion; promising to keep yourself for him and from all others until death?* How much love she would have to feel before consenting to such solemn, irrevocable vows!

She glanced to the side and caught Hayes's stare. How terrible to be linked with him. Not even to save her father could she face life as Hayes's wife. The curl of his lip showed his contempt for the sacredness of the vows that Conchita and Jim made before God and these people. Rebecca forced herself to look steadily at Hayes for a moment, refusing to show the fear that crawled in her veins, then she deliberately turned back to watch Jim place a simple gold band on his bride's finger and salute her with a quick, boyish kiss.

You couldn't do better than Scott. Smokey's satisfied announcement rang in her ears. Her heart fluttered, but a wave of people, determined to greet the bride, washed between them. Not until the new Mr. and Mrs. Jim Perkins fled to the privacy of the cabin that the Lundeens provided did Rebecca get to speak to Joel again. She found herself tongue-tied once more.

"They'll be happy," Joel said. He looked both ways and lowered his voice. "This is my first wedding."

"It was beautiful," Rebecca murmured, wondering how a man like this had escaped feminine wiles. Smokey had mentioned that Joel had passed his twentieth birthday a few months before this early summer wedding. "I look forward to hearing you preach tomorrow."

Humility replaced Joel's smile. "It's been some time since I gave a sermon, not since I left Santa Fe." He expertly guided her to a small bench partially secluded from the party that had spilled out of the adobe

192

ranch house into the yard. "I know the Lord will help me give the right message, though. He always does." Moonlight silvered his fair hair.

"Mr. Scott — or do I call you Reverend?" She laughed and nervously pleated her soft pink gown.

"Just Joel, please."

Encouraged, she asked, "Would you tell me more about your search to find your father?"

One of Joel's best skills lay in his ability to paint vivid word pictures. He told the pathetic story of his mother in a way that brought a mist to Rebecca's eyes. He mentioned his long trail to find those his uncle Gideon longed to reach with the gospel for Jesus Christ. A happy laugh crinkled his face when he said, "Just today I got word from Colorado Springs that Eb Sears and Lily are going to marry. Little Danny will have a father again, but the best thing is that Eb and Lily have decided to follow the Master. Eb is going into the store with Livingston, Lily's father-in-law, who loves her and Danny and can't bear to lose them."

"A sad tale with a happy ending. Mr., uh, Joel, do you think God has a happy ending for everyone?"

He remained quiet for several moments,

then slowly replied, "I believe everyone who accepts Christ and walks in His path will have the happiest ending of all — eternal life. I also feel God gives His children what He knows is best for them, although it may not be what we think will make us happy."

"Then, even if you don't find your father, you won't feel cheated?" It suddenly seemed vitally important to know. Rebecca clasped her hands, looked up at him in the moonlight, and added, "You won't feel that God let you down?"

"I'll be disappointed," the young minister admitted. "I still believe someday I will find Father. If I don't, God must have a reason."

Rebecca felt bitterly disappointed. "Mrs. Cook always says the same thing, that God must have a reason. If this is true, why can't He let us know?" Her fingers clenched. "I've tried to trust Him, but when I see Father growing old and going somewhere inside himself away from me, it's hard. I don't know how long it's been since he's laughed."

"Is Hayes responsible?"

The sympathetic question opened the floodgates. "He has to be. Father never was boisterous, but before Hayes came, he smiled and rode with me. Now, most of the time he just broods and lets Hayes run things. Run them down," she added. Her lips twisted. "Smokey said cattle are disappearing from the Lazy F. Then, that episode at Lone Man Cabin —" She put her hand over her mouth.

"It's all right. Smokey told me what happened."

Relief at having someone else know left her weak. "I promised not to tell Father, but I had to tell Smokey." A puzzled feeling went through her. "He said something funny tonight about maybe nailing Hayes."

Joel took her hand and pressed it. "Miss Rebecca, will you trust Smokey and me and most of all God? I have a feeling things will work out."

"Sometimes I don't think there is a way out," she said.

His fingers tightened. "There is always a way up." He freed her hand and smiled at her. "Now I'm getting into my sermon for tomorrow."

She felt her lips quiver into an answering smile but sobered when a heavy voice demanded, "What are you doin' out here?" Hayes stood at her elbow with a scowling Samuel Fairfax just behind him.

How much have they heard? Rebecca frantically wondered before she sprang to her feet. "I can't see that is any of your concern."

"It's mine." Fairfax pushed past Hayes and confronted her. "Get in the house." He turned a scorching gaze on Joel. "If I catch you around her again, I'll horsewhip you. Like father, like son."

Rebecca gasped at the sneer in his voice, the satisfaction on Hayes's face made grotesque by waving shadows that crossed and recrossed it with every movement of the rising breeze.

"I wouldn't try that if I were you." Joel leisurely got up, planted his feet apart, and did not give an inch.

"Who do you think you are!" Hayes fairly frothed at the mouth.

"Shut up, Hayes." Smokey Travis stepped from behind a cottonwood. His wedding clothes had been replaced by work shirt, pants, and vest. His Stetson rode on the back of his head, and moonlight glittered in his eyes.

Had he been playing watchdog? Rebecca felt herself go cold. "Father, Smokey, please. Don't spoil Conchita's wedding."

"That woman? I'm surprised even Perkins'd marry her," Hayes jeered. "But, he's no better than she is."

"Liar!" Smokey bellowed and dove head-first into Hayes's stomach like a barreling cannonball. The unexpected attack knocked the taller, heavier man to the ground and winded him enough so that Smokey could get in a half-dozen pounding blows on Hayes's face before Fairfax could pull him off.

"Look out!" Rebecca screamed.

Hayes had recovered enough to reach for his gun, black death in his face.

Rebecca screamed again and flung herself in front of Smokey. In the same instant, Joel, unarmed, drew back one foot and sent the gun spinning. "You rotten coward!" he said.

Smokey tore free from Fairfax and towered over Hayes on the ground, nursing a bruised hand from the powerful kick. "Next time I see you, you'd better see me first, Hayes." He whipped around toward Fairfax. "If you aren't as crooked an' yellow as this coyote, you'll kick him off the Lazy F before there ain't no Lazy F left." Rage overcame caution. "While you're at it, ask him about hawg-tying your daughter at Lone Man Cabin an' having a phony deputy who calls himself Crowley make her swear she wouldn't tell you what happened."

Father, be a man, Rebecca silently prayed — in vain. Samuel licked dry lips, sent a furious glance at the huddled figure of Hayes, cursed him, and ordered, "Get back to the ranch." His daughter saw hatred

197

beyond belief in his face, but not a word came concerning Smokey's charge.

"I told you to get in the house." Fairfax glared at Rebecca. With a little cry, she gathered her skirts around her and ran, but not before hearing Joel Scott's accusation, "Samuel Fairfax, the meanest animal alive protects its young. God forgive you for standing by and letting this vile man near the sweetest, purest girl God could create!"

His praise warmed the fleeing figure's cold heart. She slowed down before she reached the main body of merrymakers. Incredible as it seemed, they laughed, talked, and evidently had not been aware of the fight. Rebecca paused and smoothed down her hair, hoping she did not look as distraught as she felt.

"It's about time to start the shivaree," someone called. Rebecca had never been allowed to participate in the mock serenade with which cowhands often celebrated weddings. They would keep the young couple awake with their hollering, beating on pans, and demands for food.

But Rebecca could not face it now. Mrs. Cook stood a little apart, and she went straight to her. "I'm really tired. Do we have to go?"

"My stars, no, Child. Let the cowboys do

the noisemaking. We'll go on to bed. You sure looked lovely tonight. That new preacher could barely stop looking at you long enough to get Jim and Conchita hitched." A wistful look that reminded Rebecca of long-forgotten feelings crept into her face. "Joel Scott would be a solid foundation a woman could build love and a home on and know they would stand."

First Smokey, now Mrs. Cook. Rebecca wondered if she had fallen into a conspiracy to throw her into Joel's arms. The idea sent a glow through her, and long after Mrs. Cook slept, Rebecca lay awake reliving those moments on the little bench until Hayes and his evil crept into her patch of Eden.

Before daybreak, shouts and hoofbeats awakened Rebecca.

"What is it?" Mrs. Cook sleepily rose on one elbow.

Rebecca ran to the window and threw it wide open. Smokey's voice cut through the murky dawn. "Roll out, men! One of the night guard just rode in, shot to pieces. The red-and-white herd in the south pasture's gone."

"Gone?" Was that Jim Perkins's voice?

"Yeah. Gone. Vamoosed. Disappeared. Every hide an' horn of them. We're riding."

"What's going on out there?" Rebecca

199

recognized her father's bellow.

"Rustlers." Smokey's succinct reply brought action.

Ten minutes later, Rebecca had dressed, told Mrs. Cook she was going to Conchita, and joined the pale, deserted bride on the tiny porch of the cabin. Together, they watched the group of riders vanish into the predawn mists, Conchita openly crying. Rebecca's heart muscles contracted. Even the mists had not hidden a certain sunny head, bare of covering for a moment when Joel doffed his sombrero and rode away. Would there be a preaching after all? Or would some of those grim-faced riders not return? Rebecca strained her eyes until the moving black dots disappeared from sight.

"Why do men rob and kill?" Rebecca burst out. "Sometimes I hate this country."

"They have not the love of God in their hearts," Conchita sadly replied and wiped her eyes.

God. A vision of the world as it could be rose with the New Mexican sun. The day came alive in a burst of glory that failed to lift the spirits of those who watched. By mutual consent, Mrs. Cook, Rebecca, Mrs. Lundeen, and Conchita spent the waiting hours cheering one another.

"It's a shame your wedding had to be followed by something like this." Mrs. Lundeen stabbed a bright knitting needle into the ball of yarn in her lap and sighed. "Men ride off, women wait."

Conchita pressed her lips tightly together and did not answer; neither did Rebecca. Yet, time after time, one of them went for a drink of water or outside for a breath of air, but always in the direction that faced the trail that had swallowed the pursuing party.

Curly, the former Lazy F cook who now reigned in the Bar Triangle cookhouse, added fresh horror when he reluctantly crossed to the ranch house and told them that the night herder had died. "Not any older than Smokey," he said. His face contorted, and his lips thinned. He barely resembled the jolly man Rebecca remembered. "I hope they get the skunks who did this and hang them on the nearest cottonwood." His eyes slitted. "I'da gone, too, but the boy needed me worse." His shoulders sagged, and he looked straight into Rebecca's face. "Be careful, Miss," he whispered when the others considerately turned away. "Hayes didn't go with the others."

A thrill of fear shot through her. "Why not?"

"He says . . ." Curly paused. "He says Fairfax told him to keep his eyes peeled and stay here." The cook made a rude noise with his mouth.

"Do you believe him?" Rebecca demanded, hands icy with foreboding.

"Sure, just like I b'lieve the sun comes up in the west." Curly gave her another warning look and waddled back toward the bunkhouse where Hayes stood on the porch watching.

"What're you tellin' her?" Hayes held his hands menacingly close to his holsters.

"Whadda y'think I'm tellin' her?" Curly retorted. "The kid died, didn't he?"

Even with the distance between them, Rebecca could see Hayes relax. He put his hands on his wide hips and stared at her. She gave him a look of unutterable scorn and went back inside.

Yet when the men had not come back by dusk, she could no longer stand being cooped up. "I think I'll go into the courtyard," she told the others. She glanced both ways, and relieved that Hayes had ridden off earlier on some pursuit of his own, she idly walked around the flower-bright area. The perfume of roses heavily scented the evening air; the dimness before moonrise, broken only by light streaming from a few windows into the otherwise dark garden, offered respite to her aching heart. Somewhere in the vast range or forest her father, Mr. Lundeen, Smokey, and the others tracked a band of murderous rustlers who had killed once and would not hesitate to kill again. Joel rode with them, with his angelic face that could change to righteous anger, the way it had done when he defended her against her father.

Perhaps Samuel Fairfax really was not her father. If he were, how could he sacrifice her to Hayes? Or, after today, would he no longer insist she must marry against her will to save him? Surely, even though he failed to rebuke his foreman, his blind eyes must have been opened to Hayes's wickedness. Rebecca, while gazing at the splashing water in the fountain, tried to piece together the scraps of her past and Hayes's hints, the way Mrs. Cook pieced patchwork scraps until she had a complete quilt.

Lost in concentration, she forgot Conchita and Curly's warning that Hayes presented unseen danger. Suddenly, a stealthy step behind her triggered an alarm in her brain — but too late. She opened her mouth to cry out, but a rag, stuffed in her mouth, stopped her. Strong arms lifted her, too tightly for her to struggle. *God, are You there?* She clung to Joel's faith; her own was too weak to help.

CHAPTER 12

Fury flowed through Rebecca like flood-waters in autumn. How could Hayes dare to manhandle her like this? Now, she must put her anger to work and get out of this predicament. She had been warned against him but never dreamed he would be bold enough to snatch her out of the courtyard. She tried to think with his brain. Next would come a wild ride to some deserted cabin. She refused to consider anything further.

To her amazement, Hayes made no attempts to ride off with his captive. He merely carried her to an unlighted room at the far end of the sprawling ranch house and whispered in her ear, "Promise not to yell, and I'll take the gag off."

She nodded, eager to get rid of the rag or scarf or whatever it was that nearly choked her. Hayes set her down and yanked the gag. In a twinkling, Rebecca darted toward the door through which they had come. She had not promised not to escape.

"Here, none of that!" Her enemy caught her with strong hands that dug into her shoulders. She silently fought, but her 120 pounds, although range-trained to strength, could not overpower Hayes's 200 pounds. He forced her into a chair and tied her down, hands behind her back, feet crossed.

Rebecca's eyes had adjusted to the faint light that crept in through the window even before Hayes had carefully closed the shutters, struck a match, and lit a lantern. She saw he had brought her to a storeroom. Her lip curled. "I see you prepared for this outrage." She nodded at the lantern, strangely out of place among the neatly stacked boxes of supplies.

"It's time we had us a little talk," he announced. In the lantern light, he loomed taller and meaner than ever, and she hated the triumph flaming in his eyes. Had he looked like that the day he caught Conchita alone? Rebecca forced herself not to shudder. Once she showed fear, he became the master.

"There's nothing for us to discuss. Ever," she defied him, even while her bonds cut into her delicate wrists as she surreptitiously moved them to try to free herself.

Hayes lost any semblance of courtesy. "When you know everythin', you'll come crawlin' to me, beggin' me to marry you." She just stared at him, and he added, "Now you and me are goin' to settle things right now. When I rode into the Lazy F and saw you, I arranged with your daddy that we'd be married. I've kept my mouth shut waitin' to let you get used to the idea. No more. Samuel's actin' like he's about to go back on our deal and take what comes." Hayes fixed his gaze on Rebecca and laughed harshly. "It's been worth waitin'. You were a purty kid, but you're a better-lookin' woman. Too good for Travis or that young preacher."

She started, and he laughed again. "I saw him lookin' at you."

"Why don't you just say what you have to say and let me go?" Rebecca's brown eyes flashed fire, but she deliberately yawned. "I find this whole conversation tiresome."

Had she gone too far? In spite of her determination not to cringe, she could not help shrinking back when Hayes's long arms reached out as if he would shake the living daylights out of her.

"You and your haughty ways," he cried, keeping his voice low, which made it even more frightening. "Why, you ain't even

Fairfax's kid! He picked you out of some hole-in-the-wall run by outlaws, made a deal to meet your own daddy here, then murdered him, brought you to the ranch, and claimed it with some kind of paper."

Rebecca felt the blood drain from her face. Her mind churned. "It isn't true."

"You callin' me a liar? Then listen to this. If Samuel Fairfax is so pure and lily-white, how come when I rode in and accused him to his face, he turned the color of ashes and begged me to forget it?" Passion contorted Hayes's features into those of a monster bent on devouring its prey. "He offered me the foreman's job and said someday when I married you, the Lazy F would be all mine. There, that takes some of the pride outa you, doesn't it?"

It could not be true. Yet, if Hayes was lying, why had Father given him full rein over the ranch? Why did he not question the firings and unexplained cattle losses? Fairfax was not the kind of man to take such things without protest unless, as Hayes said, he had a terrible secret he feared would be discovered. Yet, something in the whole situation smelled rottener than a dead skunk. Rebecca slowly raised her chin a notch and quietly demanded, "If you're supposed to get me and the ranch anyway, just why have you been running off cattle and horses and hiding them in Lone Man Canyon?"

Hayes's face turned dirty white in the lantern light. "Who says I did that?" he blustered. "Why would I, when it's all gonna be mine real soon?"

She went cold at his confidence, but her intense gaze never wavered from his guilty face. "I worked the blindfold free, Hayes." Her voice cracked like a teamster's bullwhip. "I saw you and confirmed what I suspected when you roped and tied me. There's not an outlaw in New Mexico who'd dare touch Samuel Fairfax's daughter." Her voice broke. Perhaps she was not his daughter at all. Much as she feared to admit it, the ring of at least some truth underscored Hayes's story.

The man's gall held. "Wives can't testify against their husbands," he gloated. "Now, when that preacher comes ridin' back in . . . if he does . . . we'll have us another weddin'." He smiled.

Rebecca wondered how a smile could look so evil. Yet, with keen insight born of desperation, she saw something else. Clyde Hayes, wicked to the core, loved her. Not in the tender, gentle way she dreamed of when she thought of love, but with a love that caused him to take risks beyond belief to possess her. A flicker of an idea tickled her mind and grew. Could she play on that feeling, change it to the kind of love that would put her happiness above his own?

She stared into his face, searching for a clue, a hint of relenting or pity. She found none.

"I won't have to make you promise not to talk about this with anyone." Hayes laughed suggestively. "Men who kill in cold blood end up danglin' from a tree limb."

"The way Smokey Travis almost did — and for nothing," Rebecca bitterly accused. "Thank God Jo— Mr. Scott came when he did."

"I'll get that preacher one of these days," Hayes threatened as he untied her. "You've got 'til noon tomorrow to make up your mind whether I spill the beans and your daddy hangs." He bowed low and mockingly, swung open the door, stepped outside, and checked the courtyard. "Sleep well, Becky." His menacing laughter followed her as she ran.

Somehow, she managed to get back into the courtyard and remain long enough to gather her wits before Conchita came looking for her. The new bride's despair drove some of Rebecca's problems away when Conchita confessed, "I fear for — the men."

"Nothing too bad could have happened," Rebecca automatically consoled, noticing how large her friend's eyes looked in her pinched face. When Conchita showed no signs of being cheered, Rebecca took a deep breath and added, "We must trust in God. He is everywhere, and He can take care of Jim and Father and the others." Joel's image sprang to mind.

At last Conchita responded. Her brown fingers pressed Rebecca's tanned hand. "Gracias." But as more endless hours limped by, the strain continued. Husbands, father, friends — somewhere in the night chasing desperadoes. How could one bear it? Yet, what could not be changed must be endured. Rebecca felt she put away the last of her childhood and became a woman during the waiting time that left her too numb to even face Hayes's revelations.

The clock struck midnight. Rebecca thought she would shriek if something did not happen soon. A faint sound in the night air brought her out of her chair. "Listen!" She threw the front door wide; the steady clatter of hooves increased. Rebecca raced into the yard, closely followed by Conchita, Mrs. Lundeen, and Mrs. Cook, who had absolutely refused to go to bed while the others watched for the men.

Aware of Conchita's hard breathing beside her that echoed her own, Rebecca held her breath when a band of horses and riders swept toward them. She frantically glanced from horse to horse, then caught her throat with one hand. "Oh, God, no!"

Three of the horses wore empty saddles. One was her father's.

Joel Scott had not been asleep when the fatally wounded night herder rode in. For hours he had lain awake wondering, *Can love come this way, in two brief encounters?* Yet, he felt he had known Rebecca Fairfax always, that she had lurked in the dim recesses of his heart until he found her in reality. Everything about her pleased him. Her merry brown eyes, which could fill with horror or pain or comfort. Her tanned skin and nut-brown hair. Her sturdy form, tall enough for the top of her head to reach his lips, as she had reached his heart.

He laughed to himself. Such flights of poetry for a range-riding preacher! Yet, the intensity of her questions, when she asked if God had happy endings for people, had shown real searching for answers about God. Suddenly, his fresh-born love gave way to a higher feeling. Joel bowed his head and prayed for the girl whose rose pink gown had been no fairer than the one who wore it. His fingers strayed to the wilted rose that had dropped from her hair when she fled from her father's wrath and the ugly scene with Hayes. He had absently picked it up when the others left and tucked it in his pocket. Now he held the crumpled flower to his nose; its perfume remained intact, as alluring as Rebecca in all her innocence.

Joel still held the rose petals when the sound of a running horse shattered the predawn. One of a grim-faced group of men, he rode away to — what? Possible death, for sure. Rustlers were not known for their willingness to be captured. Memory of Rebecca's and Conchita's fearful faces when he waved to them rode with him. "God, be with us this night," he prayed, then nudged Querida closer to Samuel Fairfax and his mount. No matter what the man hid, and Joel felt sure he had a dark secret, this was still Rebecca's father. Perhaps in the long hours ahead, a time would come when he needed a friend; Smokey, Perkins, and even Lundeen seemed to have little use for Fairfax.

Smokey spurred his buckskin up alongside Joel and mumbled low enough so Fairfax could not hear, "Do you find anything funny about Hayes staying behind an' not riding with us?"

"I do." Jim Perkins must have ears like an elephant to have heard Smokey, Joel marveled. The just-married cowboy crowded close on the other side of Smokey. "Mighty peecooliar, ain't it?" He pulled his Stetson down over his forehead, and even in the pale dawn, his usually happy-go-lucky face shone sober. "Also strange that rustlers knew just what time to steal the cattle. Word didn't get sent to folks 'round here concernin' the weddin' 'til just a few days ago."

"Then someone who knew tipped the rustlers off, told them there'd just be a few cowpokes night herding," Smokey put in. This time he did not bother to lower his voice.

"What's that you say?" Fairfax spoke for the first time since they had left the Bar Triangle. "Are you accusing someone, Travis?"

"Nope. I know what it's like to be accused an' tried an' convicted when I didn't do anything." Smokey's words dropped like a shroud over the conversation. Fairfax snorted and swung away from the other three, his back stiffer than a ramrod.

Joel saw Smokey cock his head toward Jim, lift his eyebrows, then follow the owner of the Lazy F. He prodded Querida, and

Perkins's sorrel trailed after them.

"Fairfax, hold up."

The tall man reined in and glared. "What do you want?"

Smokey waited until the rest of the riders swept by before opening his coat and showing the silver badge he wore. Rays of the rising sun reflected off it.

"You? A deputy marshal?" Fairfax roared. A gray shadow crept over his face in spite of the sunlight bathing the little group huddled together.

"Shh." Smokey glanced up the trail, then back at Fairfax. "What I said last night is true. Your daughter discovered a passel of Lazy F an' other cattle an' horses all tucked away in Lone Man Canyon behind a new fence."

"Leave my daughter out of this," Fairfax ordered furiously.

"Ump-umm. Not when she ain't safe from being lassoed an' hawg-tied by crooks like Hayes an' that fake deputy Crowley."

Fairfax looked like he might explode. He licked his lips and looked sick. "I can't believe Hayes would do that! Why, when he —"

"When he thinks he's gonna get the whole kit 'n' caboodle by marryin' your daughter," Perkins tossed in.

214

Obviously shaken, Fairfax resorted to sarcasm. "When did you get on the side of the law, Travis?"

"About a week after Rebecca told me what happened at Lone Man," Smokey said quietly.

"I don't understand," Joel burst out. "All the time, when Hayes tried to hang you, why didn't you show your badge then?"

An unaccustomed red crept into Smokey's face. "Aw, I got so mad at Hayes, I yelled out what he had done to Rebecca instead of telling the boys I'd got myself appointed deputy marshal."

"You no-good dumbhead," Perkins yelled, face redder than Smokey's. "I oughta beat the stuffin' out of you here 'n' now."

Joel stopped impending hostilities by demanding, "Mr. Fairfax, I meant what I said last night. Your daughter needs protection from Hayes. If you won't give it, we will, but it's hard to believe you'll let that snake walk in and take over everything you own."

"I have no choice. If Rebecca ever finds out what Hayes knows, she'll never forgive me. You think I care about the ranch? I'd ride out with my daughter in the middle of the night if I didn't know Hayes would follow and spill everything. How can a man go

215

so far wrong?" He laughed wildly and without mirth. "Every day since Hayes rode in, my life has been miserable!" His granite face worked.

"But you don't have to go on," Joel exclaimed. Pity for the hard man suffering before him reached inside the young minister and demanded his best. "No matter what you've done, God forgives — and I believe your greathearted daughter will, too."

All the fire went out of Fairfax and left him a beaten, old-looking shell of a man. "If I could believe that, I'd . . ." He shook his head. "It's too late."

"It's never too late, Man." Joel could not let this opportunity slip away, perhaps never to come again. Yet, fate thought otherwise; the swift return of one of the posse broke into the trembling moment.

"C'mon. The tracks are leadin' to Lone Man Canyon, an' if they've got provisions, the rustlers can hole up there 'til Judgment Day!"

"Are you with us, Fairfax?" Smokey half closed his eyelids. "I got a feeling we'll find some mighty interesting things in a little while. Maybe enough to put Hayes away or hang him."

Hope flared in Fairfax's eyes, making

them bluer than usual; then it died. "I'm with you, but no matter what Hayes is accused of, it won't keep him from talking before he gets what's coming to him."

"Well, no," Jim Perkins drawled. A cheerful grin tilted his lips. "I don't reckon nobody's gonna believe much of what some rustler sez, right, Smokey? I know I wouldn't."

"Me, either." Smokey's dark eyes flashed. "Hayes can do all the crowing he wants an' just get in deeper. Trying to blackmail a well-known rancher on some trumped-up charge won't hold much water."

"If I thought that, I'd fall on my knees and thank God," Fairfax murmured. Joel saw that the tortured man really meant it. But his blood ran cold when Fairfax added, "He's insanely in love with Rebecca. It's the only thing that's kept him silent this long."

"If ya think you've been in misery, get it into your noggin that marryin' Hayes would put that daughter of yours in a whole lot more," Perkins snapped. "And she ain't done nothin' to deserve it, whether you have or not." He spurred his sorrel. "Now, ride!"

Querida leaped ahead. Joel glanced over his shoulder at Smokey and Fairfax. They followed and soon caught up with the rest of the Bar Triangle men.

"They got a head start," one angry cowboy said. He pointed to the beaten earth that bore mute evidence to the passing of a large herd of cattle. "Our man hadta ride clear back when he wasn't in no condition to do it. This ain't gonna be no Sunday school picnic." His face reddened. "Sorry, Joel. No offense 'ntended."

"None taken. Besides, sometimes even rattlesnakes come to Sunday school picnics." In an attempt to lighten the atmosphere, he added, "That's my sermon for the day, men, since we won't be home in time for the meeting."

"Haw haw." The cowboys and Lundeen roared. A faint smile even crossed Fairfax's set countenance, but the following hours wiped away everything except the knowledge that a hard and dangerous job lay ahead.

Lundeen was aghast when he saw the trail the rustlers had made no attempt to erase; he also advised caution. Once the posse reached the entrance to Lone Man Canyon, the men were to move softly and keep their eyes and ears wide open. "If we can sneak up on them all inside Lone Man Cabin, we'll order them out with their hands up. Wish we had a law officer with us." He sighed.

"We do." Smokey showed his badge. The others gasped, but Lundeen's face broke into a grim smile.

"All right. If they won't come out, we'll burn the shack. It's old and dry as tinder. Not even a rustler's gonna hang out in there once it starts smoking."

"Easy as fallin' off a horse," Perkins muttered. "But it won't be." His prediction came true. A lookout, at the top of a bluff above the canyon, sent a volley of shots down like hail.

"Take cover!" Lundeen bellowed.

Joel dove for shelter, heard heavy, running steps behind him, and twisted around. Fairfax almost made it to the screening underbrush; then he stumbled, fell. More shots rang out. To Joel's horror, Fairfax rose, twitched, and fell back. Heedless of his own safety, Joel leaped from cover and zigzagged the short distance to Samuel. He snatched him up, staggered under the heavier man's weight, and made it back to safety, vaguely conscious that Smokey and Jim had stepped into the open and emptied their rifles toward the unseen shooter.

"Is he all right?" Lundeen slithered across the needle-covered ground.

"I don't know." Joel gently laid down his burden, looked at the bright red stains that covered his hands, and shuddered. Samuel Fairfax lay broken, unconscious, and bleeding at his feet. If he died, anything he might have known about Cyrus Scott would die with him. A thought, so grotesque it made Joel's heart skip a beat, bored into his brain. *What if Rebecca wasn't Samuel Fairfax's daughter after all? What if Cyrus Scott had been that father and Fairfax knew it?*

An even more startling idea insinuated itself into Joel's mind. If such a thing proved to be true, Rebecca could never be his wife — she would be his sister.

CHAPTER 13

Lundeen examined the unconscious Samuel Fairfax with strong, sure hands, then grunted. "Ahuh. Good." He ran one finger along a shallow groove on Fairfax's head. "Creased him just enough to knock him out. Head wounds always bleed bad." He ripped his kerchief off, made a pad of it, and pressed it against the bullet wound. "Give me another scarf, someone."

Joel grabbed his from his neck and handed it over. Lundeen tore it into strips, knotted them, and wound them around Samuel's head to hold the pad in place. When he stood, his face looked stern. "All right, men, let's round up the dirty, thievin' skunks and head home. Haven't heard no more out of that sharpshooting jasper, so he's either dead or out of commission. Joel, you stay with Fairfax. It won't do for him to wake up and not know where he is. Might thrash around and start his head bleeding again.

Smokey, Jim, ride with me. The rest of you scatter and surround Lone Man Cabin. By now, I'd guess that pack of coyotes are holed up in there."

Leaving their horses tied nearby, the posse slipped through the shelter of bushes and behind trees near the cabin. Joel had not realized they were so close. By almost closing his eyes and straining, he could glimpse the dilapidated shack in the distance and hear men yelling in the clear air. He divided the eternity of waiting between checking Fairfax, who had not yet regained consciousness, and the stealthy figures closing in on the cabin.

"Come out of there with your hands up!" Lundeen's stentorian yell could almost have been heard back at the Bar Triangle.

A volley of words from the cabin answered him; a hail of bullets sang past the well-concealed posse. "Let 'em have it, boys," Lundeen roared.

A burst of gunfire and a high-pitched cry from inside the cabin brought Joel to his feet. Why was he here while Smokey and Jim and the others fought the enemy to all decent people? A terrible choice loomed. If he left his post and joined the others, in all probability he would be forced to kill, something he had vowed never to do. Sweat beaded his forehead. "God, those rustlers are vile!" Yet, Jesus had died for such as them. *What had Smokey told him so long ago?* He wrinkled his forehead. Oh, yes. He had been ready to leap up and pummel Hayes, but Smokey dragged him back into hiding and later warned, *You've gotta learn to lie still when there's danger around, no matter what.* Was God admonishing him to lie still now?

A low moan brought Joel to his knees beside Fairfax, whose hand went to his head. Joel caught it before he could disturb Lundeen's bandage. "The lookout creased you. Take it easy."

Samuel's blue eyes glazed with pain and something else. He reached toward Joel with shaking fingers.

The young minister had tended enough pain-racked persons to recognize distress. "You can talk later."

Samuel shook his head vehemently, then winced at the movement.

Sensing the fallen man's need to speak, Joel leaned close and stared straight into Fairfax's eyes. "Remember, whatever you've done, no matter how guilty you are, you can be forgiven."

A curious blend of shame, hope, and poignancy went through the watching eyes before Samuel mumbled, "Guilty . . . as . . . sin," then turned his head and closed his eyes.

Joel's heart felt like a rock. He had hoped beyond hope Fairfax would prove to be Hayes's victim and not criminally guilty. What chance did Rebecca have for the happy ending she had so wistfully confessed she dreamed of?

Lundeen's shout pierced Joel's thoughts. "Come out, or we'll burn you out," he bellowed. A sneering laugh and another round of shots served as an answer.

Joel's gaze fixed on a running figure, who carried a torch made from a dry, pitchy, pine branch. Smokey. "God, no!" Joel froze, unaware of his prayer.

The figure zigzagged toward the cabin, nimbly dodging bullets and using the cover of his comrades' heavy firing to near the cabin and toss his torch in a fiery arc that left it on the bone-dry roof and sent flames licking the tinderlike debris. Smokey veered to one side when the Bar Triangle men cheered. The cheers turned to dismay when a defiant shot from the cabin found its mark, and Smokey fell.

Hatred overrode all of Joel's caution. Heedless of the consequences, he leaped up and ran with all his might toward Smokey.

If those murderers had killed him, Joel would personally see to it they paid — unless the posse beat him to it.

Shots, dense smoke, coughing, then a loud, "We're comin' out, hands up."

"Keep them high," Jim Perkins ordered at the top of his lungs.

By the time Joel reached Smokey, seven dark-faced men, led by the so-called Deputy Crowley, had stumbled into the open, tears streaking through the soot on their faces.

"Tie them, or better yet, hang 'em," a cowboy called.

"Naw." Smokey's voice sounded surprisingly strong for a man who had been shot. He struggled to his feet, right hand pressed over his left shoulder, left hand reaching inside his coat and flashing his badge. "We'll haul them in an' let the law take care of them."

"Smokey, you're all right?" Joel grabbed his friend's arm.

"Easy, Pard. It ain't much more than a scratch, but it's sore." He scowled at the men being bound, and a wicked glint flashed in his eyes, brighter than the sun on his badge. "Play along with me," he whispered into Jim's ear, then loudly announced, "Too bad, Crowley an' the rest of you. We know who's behind our red-an'-white herd disappearing an' ending up here." He nodded past the cabin to steers crowded behind a sturdy, new-looking fence, now roiling and bellowing from the shooting. "Yeah, you notice Clyde Hayes ain't riding with us."

"Last I saw, he was standin' on the bunkhouse porch watchin' us ride off." Perkins tightened his rope around a pasty-faced Crowley.

"It wouldn't s'prise me if he's clean outa the country by the time we come ridin' in with you fellers."

"He's just the kind who'll leave someone else to take the punishment," Joel confirmed.

"That's what he thinks," one of the rustlers snarled. "He planned the raid, told us most everyone'd be up at the marryin'. I ain't takin' the blame so he c'n go free!"

"Me, neither," another put in, and a ripple of assent flowed through the group.

Crowley broke under the pressure and to save his own skin. "Hayes said Fairfax'd started actin' funny. He was afraid the old man'd go back on his word about that daughter of his, so he hired us to steal all the cattle we could before Hayes waylaid the girl and rode off with her."

Flames danced in Smokey's eyes. "You skunk! We oughta hang you right here for being part of such a scheme." He yanked out his revolver with his right hand; blood dripped down his left sleeve. Crowley's eyes looked as if he was staring death in the face.

"Get them outa here," Smokey barked and sheathed his gun. "Somebody bandage me up an' see who's hurt or dead."

Lundeen turned doctor again, while Jim and the others finished tying the outlaws in the saddles. A few minutes later, he returned to report, "One rustler's dead. Our outfit's not even scratched 'cept for Smokey 'n' Fairfax. I sent a rider up the bluff to check on the sharpshooter." That rider returned with the news the lookout man had evidently died in the exchange of shots early in the fray.

Lundeen strode back to Samuel Fairfax, who had again drifted into unconsciousness. "Hmm. It's a long ride back. Joel, you stay with him. The rest of us'll take in our prisoners and get a wagon back here as soon as we can."

"I reckon I'll stay, too," Smokey said.

"What? Let a little scratch keep you waiting for the wagon?" Lundeen joshed in his heavy manner.

"Ump-um." Unperturbed, Smokey shook his head. "Reckon you're forgetting something — Hayes." His succinct reminder snapped the men to attention. "The way I see it, soon as you ride in an' he sees his pards all trussed up like a Thanksgiving turkey, he's going to hop on the best horse he can find an' come a-running."

"He won't come this way," Joel protested. "That would be stupid."

"Naw," Perkins butted in, lean face grim. "Smokey's right. Hayes'll figure we figure that'd be just what ya said — stupid. So he'll do a double double cross and go where he ain't s'posed to be a-tall." He looked longingly at Smokey and Joel. "Lundeen, can't I stay with my pards?"

Lundeen deliberated. "You better come with me, Perkins. Just in case any of these rustlers get some funny ideas about trying to escape. With Fairfax, Joel, and Smokey missing, it leaves us shorthanded, and we've got a herd to drive, too."

"Okay, Boss." Jim heaved a big sigh, bent toward his friends, and warned, "Keep your eyes wide open. It's gonna take time to get a wagon back here. You got plenty of water from the creek. Kinda short on grub, though." He brightened. "Hey, Boss, when we knock down that fence and start the herd toward home, want me to leave a beefsteak on the hoof behind?"

Lundeen nodded. "Hurry it up. The sun

won't stick around all night, and we've got a long way to ride." The big man knelt by Fairfax, lifted an eyelid, and grunted. "He will be okay. Probably sleep and wake up a half-dozen times before we get back."

In a short time, silence replaced the cowboy yells, hoofbeats, and clouds of dust that marked the exodus of the Bar Triangle riders with their prisoners and herd.

Smokey gazed after them. "It coulda been a whole lot worse," he said significantly. He gingerly fingered his left arm. "Good thing I hit the dirt when I got winged. Say, how about some of that beefsteak? Jim hacked off a coupla hunks before he left." Smokey nodded toward the charred shack. "Lots of good embers there."

Reaction set in. Joel gulped. "I don't think I can eat anything . . . at least for awhile." He fought nausea and dropped to a downed tree trunk to hide the way his knees buckled.

"I understand." Smokey's face turned grim, and he looked older than the mountains surrounding them. "You've got to look at it this way. Let rustlers alone, an' they get bolder an' bolder. First thing you know, they start picking off honest ranchers and cowpokes, just like they did with the boy who rode out to take night watch, singing an' never knowing he'd come back all shot up." He planted both hands on his hips. "I hate killing, too. Sometimes I think a man oughta move somewhere away from every critter there is." He slowly shook his head. "Guess it wouldn't do any good. There's decent folks an' skunks no matter where you go." He grinned. "At that, let's wait awhile before we eat." He yawned. "I didn't get much shut-eye last night. Mind if I crawl under a tree an' conk out?"

"Go ahead. I'll stay with Fairfax." Joel knew he had slept even less than Smokey did, but the day's events left him wide-eyed. Besides, Fairfax might awaken and talk.

"If Hayes shows up, I'll come running," Smokey promised. "Never did sleep sound, an' since I got to be a poor, lonesome cowpoke, as Perkins calls us, I wake up real easy." He yawned again, stretched, and headed for a tall cottonwood that provided shade. Five minutes later, Joel heard snoring. He grinned. Smokey might wake easy, but he slept sounder than he admitted.

Joel gradually settled down. He drowsed until Fairfax awakened again. "Have some water." He held a canteen. Samuel drank deeply, and once more, that poignant blue light brightened his life-weary eyes. Encouraged by it, Joel asked in a low voice, "Do you want to tell me the whole story?"

Fairfax recoiled, and Joel quickly added, "About Rebecca."

The other man hesitated, then nodded. The water seemed to have cleared his mind. He brokenly began, "Rebecca's not my daughter."

Joel slowly iced in spite of the warm afternoon. What he had suspected changed to certainty. The girl he had fallen in love with must be his sister . . . and Samuel Fairfax had somehow done away with Cyrus Scott, Rebecca and Joel's father.

"I met her daddy years ago, partnered with him until he got tangled in with a band of crooked men. Hayes was one of them."

Joel's mouth dropped in astonishment, and Fairfax managed a grim laugh. "Oh, he knew me long before he came to the Lazy F. You know how he threatened to expose me. I had done nothing wrong, but I couldn't prove my innocence. Hayes only knew part of the story."

Innocence? Joel remembered the agony in Samuel's face when he had whispered, "Guilty as sin." He opened his mouth, but Samuel had already picked up the threads of his story.

Rebecca's mother had died, and her father had no choice but to keep her with him. He worshipped her, as he had worshipped her

mother. "Besides, they had no kinfolk near."
Fairfax reached for the canteen and drank
deeply again. He glanced at the still-sleeping
Smokey and lowered his voice. "When he
got in so deep with the outlaw again, my
pard came to me in the dead of night. He
told me to take Rebecca and ride out, to
get away from the breaks and head for
northeastern New Mexico. Sometime before, he'd arranged to buy a ranch."

"The Lazy F." Joel could almost see
Fairfax and young Rebecca fleeing in the
dead of night. What must that wild journey
have been like to her? His heart throbbed
with sympathy.

"The Lazy F," Fairfax confirmed. He lay
quietly for a moment, so still that the
quivering cottonwoods' secrets traveled
back and forth from leaf to leaf, as porten-
tous as those Samuel had revealed. "The
man I'd ridden with loaded me with money
and gave me ownership papers to claim the
ranch. I reasoned that even though he probably got it from stealing or worse, the girl
should have a chance. Besides, he said he'd
sneak away when he could and come. He'd
be able to travel better alone than if he had
Rebecca with him; she'd be the first person
the outlaws would look for when they followed — and they would. He never said he

helped himself to their cache, but I figured it out." Fairfax laughed grimly. "I'd found my chance to be partners, half owner of a ranch in a grand country I fell in love with years before when I rode through it. We came. Rebecca loved it, the same as me. In time, she quit asking when her daddy would come. Long before that, she'd crawled into my heart the way a son or daughter of my own would have done."

Fairfax's lips twisted. "In time, I think she forgot she wasn't mine, at least most of the time. Then, Hayes came." The man's voice changed. The look of granite returned to his face, and his eyes lost their poignant blueness. "I learned Rebecca's real daddy had been killed the very night I rode out with her! Hayes had spent all the time in between looking for me. He'd quit the gang, suspecting the truth — that I had the loot. He wandered from place to place and finally tracked me down. Said he'd swear I killed my pard to get the ranch.

"I couldn't stand for Rebecca to know her own daddy had turned outlaw or that the home she loved so much had been paid for with tainted money. I bribed Hayes to keep his mouth shut, told him he could marry Rebecca and one day own the Lazy F. He saw to it the cowboys couldn't get near her and drove them away — until Smokey came and stuck." Fairfax groaned and struggled to a sitting position, then dropped his head in his hands. "I knew she hated him, but I didn't see any other way. Then you came."

Joel held his breath and endured the searching gaze.

"You rode right in on that black horse of yours, braced me, called me, and made me look at myself. I didn't like what I saw, but I had no choice. Either I kept my word to Hayes and lost Rebecca or broke my promise that she'd marry him and lost her — forever."

"And now?" Joel leaned forward, tense as a bowstring.

"I'll go to jail, but she won't marry Hayes." Manhood flowed back into the nearly beaten man. His shoulders straightened. Some of the greatness that must once have been his came into his features. His blue eyes shone.

"That isn't necessary, Fairfax," Smokey said softly from behind them. His dark face wore a smile, blinding in its unexpected sweetness.

"What did you say?" Samuel got up from the ground, held his head, and tottered toward the cowboy. Joel's heart contracted at the look of hope that dawned in Fairfax's eyes.

"Hayes is the one going to jail for a long time, maybe forever. I've been snooping around since I got to be a deputy marshal, an' I've discovered some mighty interesting things. Such as a warrant out for the arrest of a man named Hill, who bears a curious resemblance to Hayes."

"Warrant? For what?" Fairfax shook his blood-stained head and looked bewildered.

"For the murder of Seth Foster years ago."

"Seth Foster?" Fairfax blanched and gave an awful cry. "But that's him, the man Hayes claims I killed. My pard, who bought the Lazy F under the name Samuel Fairfax!"

"Correct." Smokey grinned, took the makings from his shirt pocket, and rolled a cigarette. He stuck the brown paper cylinder into his mouth, lit it, and puffed once.

Joel felt he had wandered into a never-ending maze. Seth Foster . . . Samuel Fairfax . . . Hayes who was really Hill. He shook his head. Once, he had been caught in rolling, red floodwaters. Their turgid undercurrents had threatened to suck him under and hold him until life fled. Now he felt caught the same way, tossed by dark currents he could neither understand nor fight. "Then Rebecca Fairfax is really Rebecca Foster?"

235

"I took his name to claim the ranch, the way he insisted. The transaction had been through another party, one who knew nothing of Seth's real name." Fairfax clutched his head and sat back down on the ground. "Can you see why I didn't want Rebecca to know all this, when I could prove nothing except that I traveled under a dead man's name, had that man's daughter, and lived on a ranch he owned?"

A million questions danced in Joel's beleaguered brain. Yet foremost, relief underlined each. Rebecca was not his sister. Gladness like a prayer winged into Joel's heart.

"Hold the confab," Smokey warned and ran toward a vantage point to return a few minutes later wearing a broad grin. "It's okay. Thought I heard something."

"They won't get a wagon back before tomorrow," Fairfax predicted. "Did I hear something about beefsteak, or was I dreaming?"

"I fry a mean piece of meat," Smokey admitted. "Pard, you feel like eating now?" he asked Joel.

The young minister only nodded. All his questions had come down to one burning thought, something between him and Fairfax, not even to be heard by the faithful

Smokey. With a keen glance, that worthy individual grinned and walked away to fry his steak.

"Mr. Fairfax, no, that isn't your name, is it?" Joel tried to find his way out of the maze. "Oh, hang it all, if you aren't Fairfax, who are you?" His voice sounded loud in his ears, but he knew it would not carry past the first tattletale cottonwood. "And what do you know about Cyrus Scott? *I have to know*." He braced himself for the truth, prepared for anything — except Fairfax's answer.

Quietly, without fanfare, the older man stared straight at Joel. "I am Cyrus Scott, your father."

CHAPTER 14

"I am your father," the man that Joel had known as Samuel Fairfax repeated.

"God forgive me."

Faced by the shocking end of his long search, the younger man could only stare. All these weeks, the father he had sought for months, right here. "But you said he probably died years ago," Joel stammered.

The poignant light he had come to recognize but never understood crept again into the Lazy F's owner's eyes, turning them so blue, Joel wondered how he could have failed to identify this man as a Scott.

Joel felt his own eyes burn when his father said, "I tried to bury Cyrus Scott years ago after I discovered your mother died. If I'd only known about you!" The anguished cry tore into Joel's heart.

"You couldn't know. Judith was afraid you'd take me."

Cyrus flinched. "Once, I would have." He

238

raised a shaking hand. "Can God forgive me? Can you?" His eyes looked like those of a dog Joel once rescued from a beating.

Everything the young minister believed about forgiveness battled with his long-standing hurt and anger at what Cyrus had done. He had prattled of the need to forgive without knowing the depths of his own resentment or the difficulty of doing so. Now, his father's question nailed him to the cross of memories. If he could not forgive, Cyrus would never believe God could, either.

Slowly, almost of its own volition, Joel's hand extended, and for the first time, he touched his father . . . tentatively, then with a hard grip of hands that promised much. Joel felt Cyrus's fingers tremble. A look of near-glory cut years off Cyrus's face until he resembled Gideon. Joel took a sharp breath. A flood of pent-up emotions roared through him.

"Hey, steaks are done an' burning," Smokey called.

After another mighty squeeze, the two men's hands parted. Shoulder to shoulder, they headed toward Smokey. When they reached him, Joel threw back his head and announced, "I'd like you to meet my father."

Smokey gave them an inscrutable look. "I know."

"What?" Joel leaped toward him and glared. "You know?"

"Sure. When I got to nosing around, I put a few facts together an' figured it out." His maddening smile drove Joel wild, especially when he added with a grin that stretched clean across his face, "The way I see it, 'til your daddy got ready to talk, it was up to me to button my lip an' keep it that way."

"Thanks, Smokey." Cyrus offered his hand to the cowboy he had driven off his ranch.

In the greatheartedness that set Smokey apart from the common herd, he responded and shook heartily before complaining, "If we don't eat, this beefsteak's gonna be tougher than saddle leather."

The three men fell to and finished every scrap of the enormous steak, then chafed at the bit until the wagon from the Lazy F arrived. Lundeen and his men had taken the two dead rustlers' horses and the one Cyrus had ridden back to the ranch with them. Now, Smokey on his buckskin and Joel on Querida trailed the team and wagon, along with Jim Perkins, who had changed horses and come back.

"I'm glad we ain't hauling Rebecca's

daddy back worse hurt than he is," Smokey muttered. He cocked an eyebrow. "Say, Pard, since she won't ever love me the way a woman should, I hope you get her."

Joel marveled at the unselfish loyalty of the man whose life he had saved. "I do, too."

Smokey yawned. "Me for the bunkhouse soon as we get there." The next moment, he straightened out of his slumped position. "Dust cloud over there."

Jim glanced in the direction Smokey pointed. "So what?"

"That's the direction of the Lazy F, Dumbhead," Smokey retorted.

Perkins pulled his Stetson farther down over his eyes. "He's had just about enough time to get to the Lazy F and back."

"Who?" Joel sensed significance in the exchange. "You mean Hayes?"

Jim snorted disgust. "I ain't the only dumbhead around here even if you are a preacher." He narrowed his eyelids and cried, "Will ya look at what he's ridin'?"

Joel concentrated on the distant moving dot.

"By the powers, if that's not Vermilion!" Smokey snapped his spine straight and raced to the wagon driver. "Hayes is heading back toward Lone Man riding Vermilion. Tell the boss we're following him." He wheeled his buckskin and galloped the way they had come. "Come on, pards. We may be able to head him off. Joel, we've been wanting to see what that Kay-reeda horse of yours can do. Now's the time!"

A thrill of adventure shot through Joel. Querida responded to the change of directions with her usual grace. Jim and Smokey could not have kept up if Joel had not held Querida in. She might need her magnificent reserve of strength later rather than at this moment.

Taking advantage of a line of cottonwoods in between, the three riders managed to stay out of Hayes's sight until just before they reached Lone Man. They flashed into the open, then saw Hayes look their way, check the big red stallion that fought him, and take off toward the north.

"I knew Vermilion'd never stand for that skunk," Smokey yelled. "Rebecca an' me are the only ones he takes to."

"Good." Perkins's mouth opened in a wide grin. "Ride 'em, cowboys!" He bent low over his horse's neck and urged her closer, taking care not to crowd Querida with her flying hooves.

A long, straight path lay before them, with Vermilion racing straight for the mountains. Hayes had evidently mastered the stallion temporarily and put him into a dead run.

Smokey sped up until he could shout to Joel, "We can't catch him. Maybe you can. He ain't taking time to use his rifle. He probably cleaned out all the cash an' jewels he could find at the Lazy F an' figures on hiding out. Querida, show your stuff!" He snatched the sweat-stained Stetson from his head, leaned over, and cuffed Querida's flank.

Unused to being struck, the soot-black horse whinnied in protest, gathered her muscles, and gave a mighty spring. She came down stretched out and already into the gliding run that won admiration from anyone who saw her race.

Joel heard the loud "Whoopees" from Smokey and Jim. He looked over his shoulder at them pelting along behind as fast as their mounts could carry them, then slipped into his forward thrust position and called in Querida's ear, "Go, Beloved!"

A half mile later, Joel knew he had gained on Vermilion and Hayes, but not much. Another half mile and the distance between them shrank, but infinitesimally. At the end of two miles, Querida's flowing stride narrowed the space between them until Hayes rode glancing back over his shoulder every few minutes.

Joel knew Querida and Vermilion were equally matched. Under the same conditions, the outcome of the race would be a toss-up. Today, Querida had the advantage of nearly a day's rest and grazing against the long ride Vermilion had already made from the Lazy F.

Now, Joel came close enough to see Hayes's hate-filled face and the way he rudely raked the red stallion's sides with his spurs. "Don't do it!" he wanted to shout. Obviously, Hayes did not realize what such treatment of a high-spirited mustang would do, a horse that had never known spur or whip and had been tamed with love and kindness.

In desperate straits, with Querida closing in on him and Smokey and Jim galloping nearer all the time, Hayes lost his wits completely. He spurred Vermilion again. At the same time, he transferred the reins to his left hand and reached with his right to his rifle scabbard to jerk out his weapon.

With a horrid scream, Vermilion retaliated. Instead of running faster, he leaped into the air, whirled, and came down on stiff legs. It jolted the rifle from Hayes's hand. He snatched for it, missed, and threw himself off balance.

For the second time, Vermilion bucked,

jerking the reins free of Hayes's restraining grip and getting his head between his knees. Humped like an upside down "U," the red horse came to earth in a series of bone-crunching leaps and dislodged his rider.

To Joel's horrified gaze, Hayes fell heavily — but his left ankle twisted in the stirrup. He kicked frantically, trying to free himself. Joel screamed at Querida to run; Smokey and Jim thundered behind them, too late.

Not until Vermilion worked himself free of the dragging man, did he, at Smokey's urgent whistle, halt and stand trembling while the cowboy he loved calmed him down and tethered him to a nearby cotton-wood.

"Hayes?" Smokey asked, his face gray.

"Dead." Joel turned away from the man who had plotted against others, murdered Rebecca's father, and now lay at their feet, a victim of his own evil. Sick of it all, he buried his face in Querida's sweating side and stayed a long time. When he turned, he saw Jim slip a roll of greenbacks into his saddlebag with the comment, "Reckon Fairfax'll be glad to get this."

Joel shuddered, but Smokey looked first at him, then at Jim, last of all at the red stallion that stood quietly, his nose nudging Smokey's shoulder. "We have to tell folks

Vermilion threw Hayes." The gray shade had not lifted from his face. "He's no killer horse, though. An' if Rebecca knows just how Hayes died, she won't ride or trust Vermilion."

"No reason she should know, is there?" Jim's intent gaze bored into Joel.

Joel shook his head, unable to believe the docile creature that trotted after Smokey like a pet dog could have been transformed into a whirling cyclone from sheer pain and mistreatment.

"Then we don't tell her a-tall." Jim sighed. "You'll have to let Querida race Vermilion sometime, Joel, or folks won't believe she beat him."

"It wasn't a fair race," Joel quietly told them. "Vermilion had been ridden miles and miles before it began." He stared at the long, still figure covered by a tarp from Jim or Smokey's saddle. "How do we get him back? I doubt that Vermilion will stand for carrying him."

"The buckskin will." Smokey and Jim hoisted the tragic burden to the horse's broad back and secured it. "I'll ride Vermilion soon as he gets his wind."

Drained by the revelations and events of the past few days, Joel simply let the reins lie loose and left it to Querida to follow the trail home. Smokey and Jim rode behind him, but the minister who no longer felt young did not look back. Behind him lay the ghastly reminder that the wages of sin is death. Only by looking forward could he rid himself of the bloodshed and violence. No wonder Jesus wept over the world and commanded His followers to tell others of Him and free them from darkness.

Hours earlier, when the clock at the Bar Triangle struck midnight, Rebecca heard hoofbeats, and the waiting women ran into the yard. A gang of horses and riders swept toward them. Three of the horses wore empty saddles; one was Samuel Fairfax's.

"Oh, God, no!" Rebecca caught her throat with one hand. "Father?"

"He's gonna be all right, Miss Rebecca." Jim Perkins leaped from his sorrel, gathered a sobbing Conchita in his arms, and smiled at Rebecca over the bowed, dusky head.

"But where is he?" She frantically checked the group of men surrounding a sullen-faced band of bound men. "And Joel? And Smokey?"

"All right as sunshine in the mornin'." Nothing daunted Perkins for long. "Your daddy got creased, head wound. Made him too dizzy to ride. We're sendin' a wagon for him soon as it gets light. Joel 'n' Smokey stayed with him."

"You're sure Father isn't badly hurt?"

Jim shoved back his Stetson, and the light streaming from the open doors behind them shone on his face. "Lundeen says he's okay, and Lundeen knows about doctorin' — he patched up your daddy's head." The reassurance in his voice gave way to a sudden frost. "Where's Hayes? Turns out he's behind all this mess."

"I heard a horse goin' out as we were comin' in," a cowboy sang out. "Want us to go get him?"

"Naw. He won't know for sure if we're onta him." Perkins gave a mighty yawn. "It ain't long 'til daybreak. Get some shut-eye, and we'll go chasin' Hayes tomorrow." He turned Conchita toward their new home, and they walked away, his arm around her shoulders, hers on his waist.

Rebecca watched them through a mist of envy. If God ever allowed her to walk that way with Joel . . . She shook her head, and when she got back inside, went to her room, unwilling to talk even with Mrs. Cook. The shock of seeing that riderless horse and noticing Joel had not come home had unnerved her.

"God," she prayed. "You win. Even if

Father is hurt worse than Jim said or if Joel never loves me, You can help me. No one else can. No matter what happens, please, accept and be with me." Surprisingly enough, she fell into such a deep sleep that she never heard when the wagon went for her father but awakened to sun streaming into the room and a feeling of hope inside her.

The hope wavered when she saw how worn her father looked, the bloody bandage around his head. Not until he held out a hand and said, "Daughter, as soon as I get cleaned up, I want to talk with you," could she believe he really would get well. Yet, the following talk — in which he freely confessed his wild youth, real identity, and how her own father had died — brought her pain beyond belief for the white-faced man who spoke, for the weak, easily led father, for the mother she could barely remember.

Cyrus finished by telling her, "Joel has forgiven me. I believe God will, too." He turned his face toward the west. "One day, we'll go find Gideon and Judith and my parents." His voice faltered, and he brushed his hand across his eyes. "Joel says they forgave me long ago. Can you? My only excuse is that I loved you as the child I longed for."

Tears gushed. She flung herself into his arms as she had longed to do since childhood. "You're the only father I've ever known. The name doesn't matter."

"Especially when it appears to me a certain young minister and newly discovered son of mine intends to convince my adopted daughter that Rebecca Scott's a much nicer name than Rebecca Foster-Fairfax!" His blue eyes twinkled, and color returned to his gaunt face.

"Rebecca, you run along now and let your daddy rest," Mrs. Cook ordered from the doorway. If she had heard Cyrus's comment, she chose to ignore it as well as the rich blush that crept into the girl's fresh face.

Banned, Rebecca fled to her room, then sallied forth to watch for Joel, Jim, and Smokey. Her heart had flip-flopped when the driver of the wagon carrying Cyrus told her sourly, "Those three took off like skeered jackrabbits after Hayes. They should be 'long most any time."

Any time stretched into hours, but at last Rebecca's peering from the window rewarded her. Three drooping horses with tired-looking riders rode into view. Conchita, who had joined Rebecca's vigil, exclaimed, "There are four horses. What —"

Rebecca did not wait for the rest of her sentence. She bounded outdoors in spite of the dress she wore in place of her usual riding clothes. She had put it on, refusing to admit even to herself how much she longed for Joel to notice and approve. "Vermilion?" She halted just outside the corral. "Smokey — what — who — ?" She mutely pointed toward the tarpaulin-covered figure the men slid to the ground.

Smokey waited until they finished, then doffed his hat. "He took all the cash he could find at the Lazy F. Thought he'd get away, probably leave New Mexico territory."

"What happened to him? You didn't shoot him, did you?" Rebecca clenched her hands and looked pleadingly from Smokey to Jim to Joel. He looked at her with such compassion in his eyes that she suddenly felt afraid. "Smokey, tell me."

"Aw, he couldn't handle Vermilion. Tried to run away from Querida, who was fresh." Smokey awkwardly turned the big hat in his hands. "Vermilion threw him and he landed bad."

Relief flowed through her. "Thank God! I couldn't stand for you to have killed him." She shuddered and involuntarily looked at Joel.

A beautiful light dawned in Smokey's tired

face. "We appreciate that. Now, we're three dirty tramps who need baths. If you'll excuse us, I reckon we'll see you later." He limped off, bearing evidence of long hours in the saddle. Jim followed, but Joel lingered.

"Have you talked with . . . your father?"

She smiled tremulously. "My adopted father has told me everything." She remembered Cyrus's final statement and turned rosy red.

"May I see you later?" he asked in a low tone.

"Why, of course." Her traitorous heart nearly gave her away.

"In the courtyard, perhaps?" His blue eyes so like his father's eloquently presented his unspoken cause.

"Not in the courtyard." She bit her lip. "Last night Hayes caught me there and . . . and threatened me." Later, she could tell him the whole story. Now, she moved in a daze through the hours between his homecoming and the end of the supper hour. Clad in white, a rose tucked in her hair, Rebecca glimpsed herself in a mirror, gasped, and leaned closer. *Had love made her beautiful?* Her usually merry brown eyes had softened; her skin glowed. The curves of her red lips looked fuller. *Or had surrender to her Lord added the finishing touches?*

252

Joel led her away from the lighted ranch house, down toward the river that rippled in the starlight. Columbine and bluebonnets bent their heads when the couple passed. A knowing moon cocked one eye and turned Joel's blond hair to glistening silver; it reflected in Rebecca's eyes.

Joel found a smooth stump, brushed it clean, and seated her. "Rebecca," he said softly. "I think I've been looking for you all my life. Could you ever care for me?"

A rush of unworthiness filled her. "I . . . I can never be good enough for you, a man of God." Her voice sounded small and forlorn in the big night. "Though now I know you're right . . . no one can live and be happy without Him." She drew in a long breath and released it. "I told Him that today before you came home." She ignored his involuntary start and quickly added, "I didn't bargain. I just . . . accepted."

"I am so glad." Joel hesitated. "Love isn't a matter of being good enough. It's sharing and growing. I love you more than anything on earth. Do you care at all?"

"I care." Her low whisper reached his ears. He caught her close, never to let her go. She nestled in his arms, heard his heart beat, and felt more protected than ever before in her life.

Later would come all the explanations, the long trip back to San Scipio and the Circle S, and a much longer trip to the Double J, their new home in Arizona. For now, green leaves fluttered above them, whispering in the wilderness their secrets of love and joy and the gospel of Jesus Christ that they would carry.

But Perkins, the incorrigible, had the last word. Walking with his new wife in the moonlight, they paused and observed the charming tableaux that Joel and Rebecca made posed under the cottonwoods. Jim tightened his arm on Conchita's shoulders and whispered, "Snappin' crocodiles, looks like we'll be havin' another weddin'. Say, Connie, how'd ya like to see Arizona? It's a shame for pards like me 'n' Joel 'n' Smokey to get broke up." He snickered real low and added, "Besides, I bet some Arizona gal's just waitin' to meet some cowpoke like Smokey. Ain't it our duty to see she ain't disappointed?"

Conchita dragged him away and left the night to Joel, Rebecca, and the still-whispering trees.

Dear Readers,

I hope you enjoy reading *Whispers in the Wilderness,* the second title in the FRONTIER BRIDES series as much as I enjoyed writing it. My parents had a deep love for reading and western history. They passed it on to my brothers and me. One Christmas during hard times Mom splurged and bought Dad twenty Zane Grey books. The $14. gift provided many happy hours reading by kerosene lamp light.

After World War 2 ended and money wasn't so tight, we camped all over the western states and saw places we already knew from Zane Grey's accurate descriptions. Those trips strengthened my desire to write western novels "someday."

"Someday" came years later when in 1977 I felt called to walk off my government job and write full-time. Now, with six million copies of my 140+ "Books You Can Trust" sold, I marvel. God chose an ordinary logger's daughter to help make the world a better place by providing inspirational reading.

May the FRONTIER BRIDES series bring

a smile, a tear, inspiration, and hope to each
of you.

In His Service,
Colleen L. Reece